SPECIAL THANKS: JESSE POST,
STEVE BEHLING, KELLY BONBRIGHT,
ROB TOKAR AND BRYCE VANKOOTEN

FIRST EDITION: SEPTEMBER 2010

10 9 8 7 6 5 4 3 2 1

FOR INFORMATION REGARDING THE CPSIA ON THIS PRINTED MATERIAL CALL: 203-595-3636 AND PROVIDE REFERENCE # EAST – 68031

Office of publication: 6310 San Vicente Blvd Ste 404, Los Angeles, CA 90048-5457.

A catalog record for this book is available from OCLC and on our website www.boom-kids.com on the Librarians page.

WRITERS:

JESSE BLAZE SNIDER (CHAPTERS 1-3)
JAKE BLACK (CHAPTER 4)

ARTISTS:

TANYA ROBERTS (CHAPTERS 1-3)
DIEGO JOURDAN (CHAPTER 4)
TRAVIS HILL (CHAPTER 1, PGS 1-5; CHAPTER 3, PGS 1-4)

COLORS:

MIKE COSSIN
WITH **ERIC COBAIN** (CHAPTER 1, PAGES 1-5)

LETTERS:

DERON BENNETT (CHAPTERS 1 & 3)
TROY PETERI (CHAPTERS 2 & 4)

COVER ART: NATHAN WATSON
COLORS: MIKE COSSIN

ASSISTANT EDITOR: JASON LONG
EDITORS: CHRISTOPHER MEYER & AARON SPARROW
DESIGNER: ERIKA TERRIQUEZ

CHAPTER ONE
Hold your fire, men!
BUKITAKUS has Bo Peep!
She'll be fine! Fire away!
Belay that order, soldiers!

Forget about me! Please, somebody... save my sheep!!!

BAAAAAHHHH!!!

Hold your ground, men! Reinforcements are on the way!

Eh, if this thing eats lamb chops, I'm taking pork off the menu!
That goes double for baked Potato Heads!

WHAM!!!
COUGH!

WHUMP!

It's BUZZ LIGHTYEAR!!!!

Run for it!
WAAH!
Poit!
Oof!
That was a close shave!
You're telling me?!
YOW!

WHUD

Too many accessories to live, too marketable to die! Say somethin', Potato!
My mouth is over here!

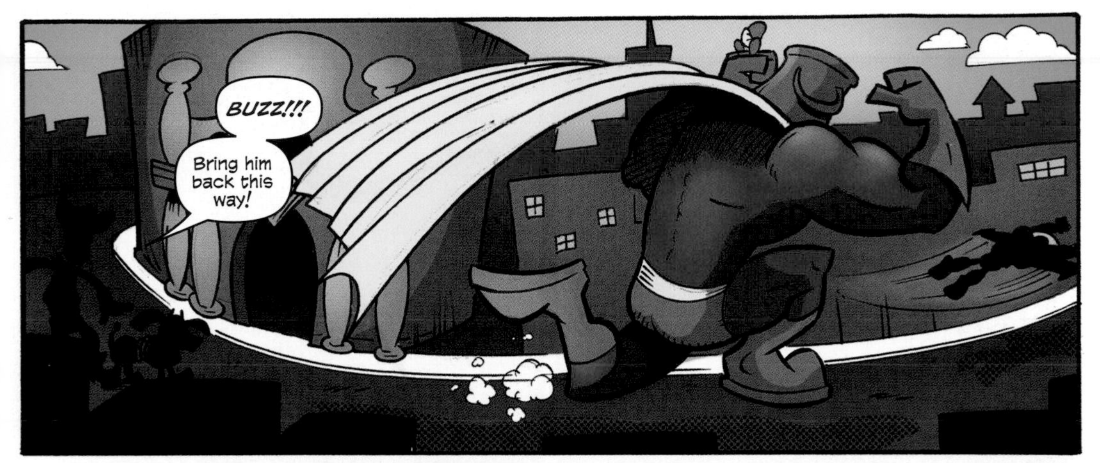
BUZZ!!!
Bring him back this way!

Reading you loud and clear, Woody!
If you just tell me where you wanna go, I'll make sure I'm not there!!!
You know what to do, Slink?!
You betcha, Woody!

I'll save you, Bo PEEEEEEEEEP!!!

Be gentle!

TIMBER!

Great idea, Woody!
THUMP!
Thanks, Buzz! But it was Slinky that brought down the beast!
Thank you both so much for saving my sheep!
It was nothing, ma'am.
Now let's hogtie this monster, before he wakes up!
That's right, all in a day's work for the team of Buzz and Woody!
ANDY?!
YEAH?!
I HAVE TO GO TO THE STORE! AND THAT MEANS YOU TOO!
CAN WE AT LEAST GET PIZZA FOR DINNER?!
MAYBE...!
HUFF... OKAAAY...!

ARGH!
COME HERE, YOU!

OH, HELLO, MISS PEEP.
YOU CAN CALL ME, "BO."
AH...BO. WHAT CAN I DO FOR YOU?

I WANTED TO THANK YOU, BUZZ...FOR SAVING MY FLOCK.
OH, WELL... ALL IN A DAY'S WORK, MA'AM...
WELL, I HAVE TO REWARD YOU SOMEHOW.

REWARD...? UM...

HEY, HEY, HEY, WAIT A SECOND!
HE DIDN'T *ACTUALLY* SAVE YOUR SHEEP! IT WAS ALL PART OF ANDY'S GAME!

BESIDES, IF *ANYONE* SAVED YOUR SHEEP, IT WAS *ME!* DID YOU SEE THAT LASSO WORK?!
OH, WOODY! THERE'S NO NEED TO BE JEALOUS, I'M JUST BEING FRIENDLY!

WHAT?! I'M NOT JEALOUS! IT'S JUST...YOU KNOW...IF I HADN'T BEEN THERE, THOSE SHEEP WOULD HAVE GONE *SPLAT* ON THE FLOOR!
"SPLAT ON THE FLOOR," WOODY?

ALL I'M SAYING, BUZZ, IS THAT IF ANYONE DESERVES A THANK YOU KISS AROUND HERE, IT'S *ME!*
OH PLEASE! IF NOT FOR MY TIMELY ARRIVAL, THOSE SHEEP WOULD HAVE BEEN SWALLOWED BY *BUKITAKUS!*
REALITY CHECK, GENTLEMEN!

"BUKITAKUS" IS *ANDY!* NEITHER ONE OF YOU DID *ANYTHING!*
A LITTLE BOY DRESSED AS A SPACE GIANT CONTROLLED YOUR EVERY MOVE, AND DECIDED THE ULTIMATE FATE OF *EVERYONE!*
IF ANYONE DESERVES A KISS IT'S *ME* FOR NOT BEING COMPLETELY *DELUDED!*
AND JUST WHO WOULD BE *GIVING* YOU THIS KISS?!

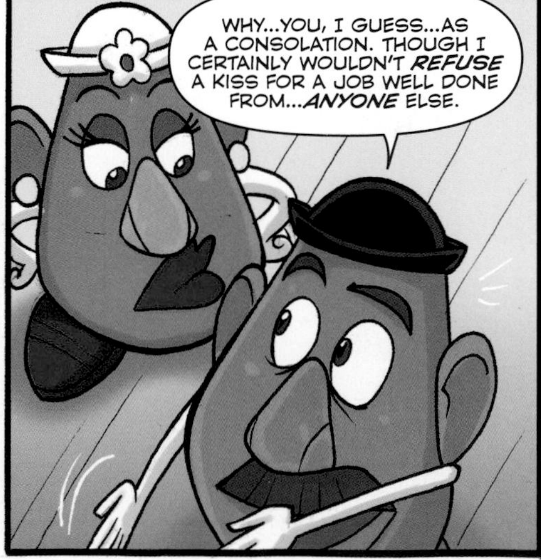
WHY...YOU, I GUESS...AS A CONSOLATION. THOUGH I CERTAINLY WOULDN'T *REFUSE* A KISS FOR A JOB WELL DONE FROM...*ANYONE* ELSE.

MWAH
I STAND CORRECTED.

MUCH AS I HATE TO ADMIT IT...POTATO IS *RIGHT*. WE'RE BEING RIDICULOUS. NEITHER ONE OF US DESERVES A REWARD.
GREAT! SO, CAN WE JUST—
SO I SAY...WE *FIGHT* FOR IT!
WHAT?!

ARE YOU PROPOSING A *DUEL*, COWBOY?
NO...A *CONTEST!* AN ACTION FIGURE FACE OFF WITH OBSTACLE COURSES AND CHALLENGES! WINNER GETS A *KISS* FROM BO.
HEY! I DIDN'T AGREE TO--
I'M IN.
I'M IN!

OOH! ME TOO! I *HATE* BEING LEFT OUT OF THINGS!
1000111111!
IN.
SOUNDS LIKE FUN!

WELL, I GUESS IF EVERYONE *ELSE* IS DOING IT, I DON'T HAVE MUCH CHOICE...
OH, YOU "HAVE TO," HUH? WELL, THEN YOU DESERVE EVERYTHING YOU'RE ABOUT TO GET!

KISS!!!

FREE KISSES...FREE KISSES...FREE KISSES...
Free Kisses
FREE KISSES... FREE

DO YOU THINK I SHOULD LOWER MY PRICE?
YES. YOU... PAY...US...
Free Kisses
YES!...

WOODY...
ACTION
1ST PRIZE
KISS FROM
ALL RIGHT, EVERYONE, LET'S KEEP THE LINE ORDERLY! JUST SIGN-UP HERE, REX...
BOY HOWDY, THIS IS EXCITIN'!

WOODY... WE NEED TO TALK.
SURE BO, JUST GIVE ME A MINUTE.

NOW, WOODY!
OW!

HEY, OUCH! WHAT'S THE PROBLEM?!
YOU'RE THE PROBLEM, WOODY! YOU'RE EMBARRASSING ME WITH THIS! I DIDN'T AGREE TO THIS!
WHAT'S TO BE EMBARRASSED ABOUT BO? EVERYONE LOVES YOU!

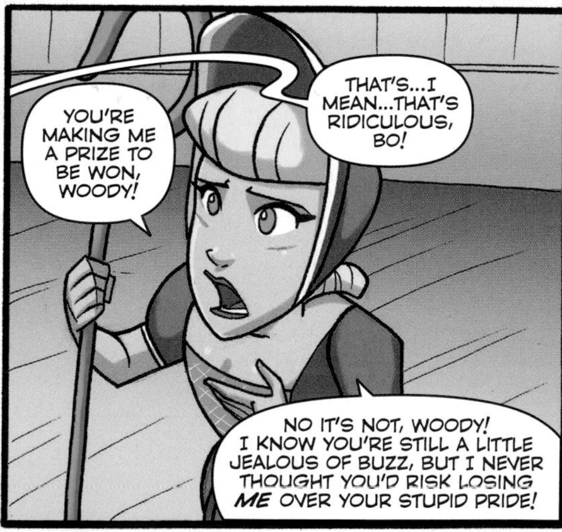
YOU'RE MAKING ME A PRIZE TO BE WON, WOODY!
THAT'S...I MEAN...THAT'S RIDICULOUS, BO!
NO IT'S NOT, WOODY! I KNOW YOU'RE STILL A LITTLE JEALOUS OF BUZZ, BUT I NEVER THOUGHT YOU'D RISK LOSING ME OVER YOUR STUPID PRIDE!

I'M NOT GONNA LOSE YOU, BO. BECAUSE I'M NOT GOING TO LOSE!
YOU'D BETTER NOT...BECAUSE I WON'T BE HERE WAITING IF YOU DO.

BO...!

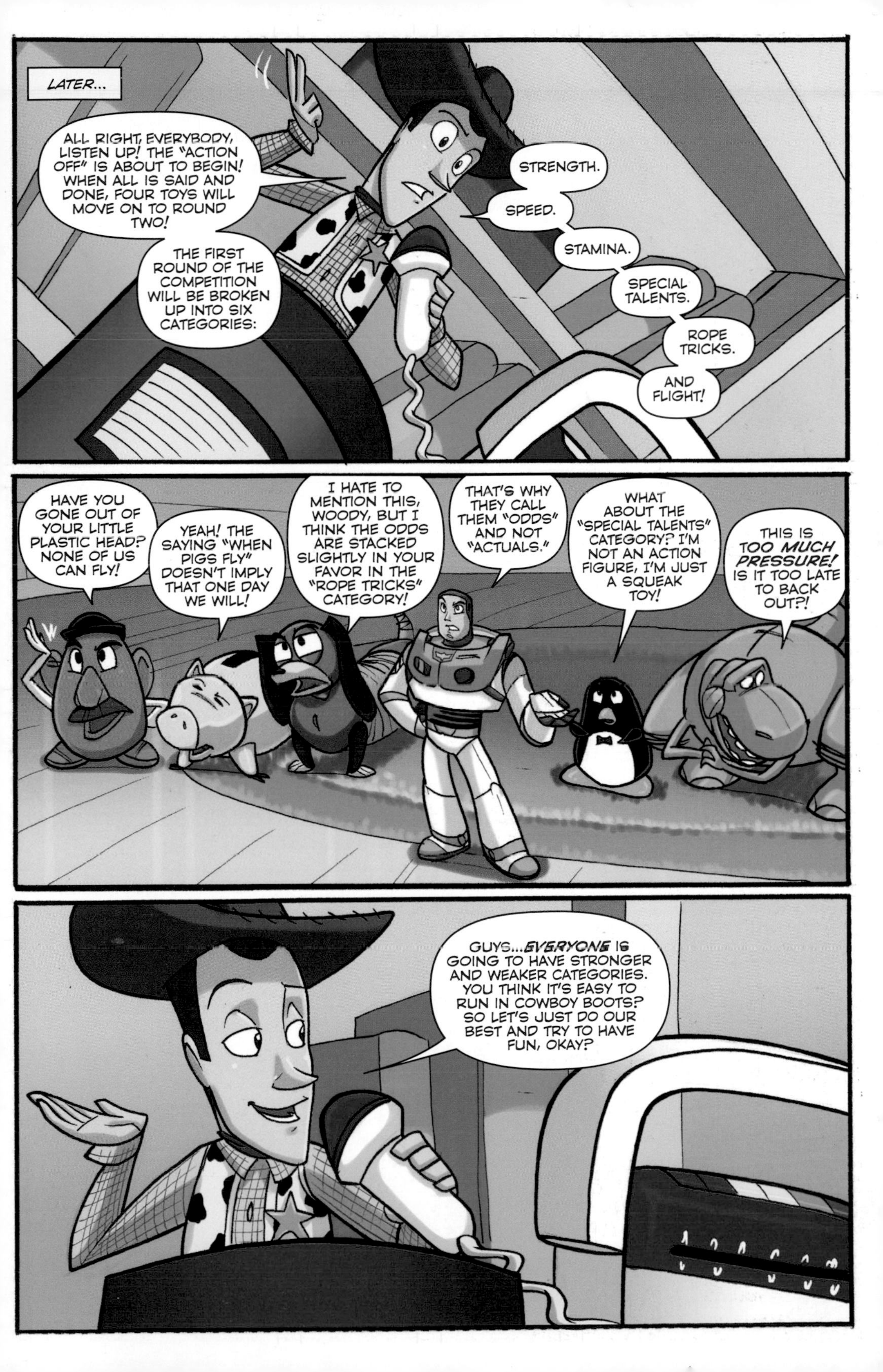
LATER...
ALL RIGHT, EVERYBODY, LISTEN UP! THE "ACTION OFF" IS ABOUT TO BEGIN! WHEN ALL IS SAID AND DONE, FOUR TOYS WILL MOVE ON TO ROUND TWO!
THE FIRST ROUND OF THE COMPETITION WILL BE BROKEN UP INTO SIX CATEGORIES:
STRENGTH.
SPEED.
STAMINA.
SPECIAL TALENTS.
ROPE TRICKS.
AND FLIGHT!
HAVE YOU GONE OUT OF YOUR LITTLE PLASTIC HEAD? NONE OF US CAN FLY!
YEAH! THE SAYING "WHEN PIGS FLY" DOESN'T IMPLY THAT ONE DAY WE WILL!
I HATE TO MENTION THIS, WOODY, BUT I THINK THE ODDS ARE STACKED SLIGHTLY IN YOUR FAVOR IN THE "ROPE TRICKS" CATEGORY!
THAT'S WHY THEY CALL THEM "ODDS" AND NOT "ACTUALS."
WHAT ABOUT THE "SPECIAL TALENTS" CATEGORY? I'M NOT AN ACTION FIGURE, I'M JUST A SQUEAK TOY!
THIS IS TOO MUCH PRESSURE! IS IT TOO LATE TO BACK OUT?!
GUYS...EVERYONE IS GOING TO HAVE STRONGER AND WEAKER CATEGORIES. YOU THINK IT'S EASY TO RUN IN COWBOY BOOTS? SO LET'S JUST DO OUR BEST AND TRY TO HAVE FUN, OKAY?

STRENGTH: THE BENCH PRESS
NO ONE'S GOING TO TOP THI-- HUH?!

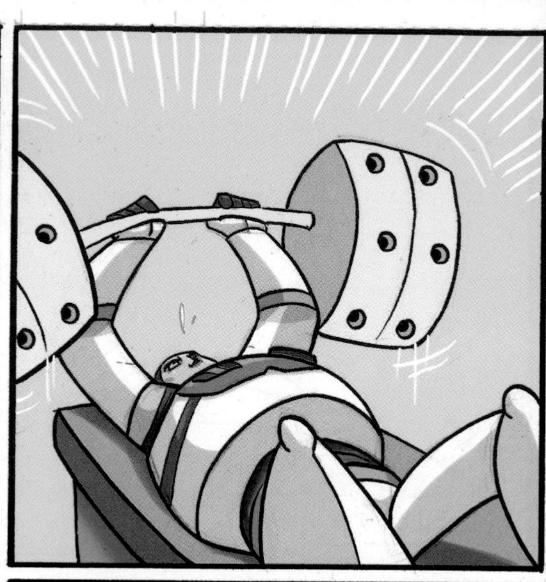

ANOTHER 250 REPS! HUP TWO THREE FOUR...

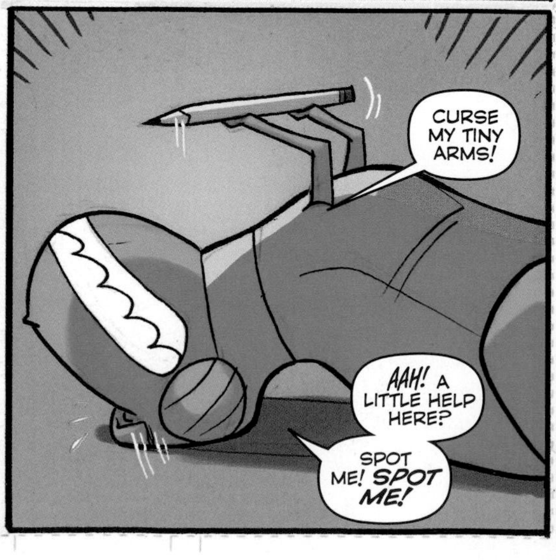
CURSE MY TINY ARMS!
AAH! A LITTLE HELP HERE?
SPOT ME! SPOT ME!

SPEED: THE TWENTY FOOT DASH
READY...
SET...
YOU REALLY THINK YOU'VE GOT A SHOT, COWBOY? I JUST BEAT A BRAND NEW TOY LAST WEEK!*
YEAH, BUT AS YOU SAID, OLD TOYS HAVE LOOSE LEG JOINTS, AND I'M A PRETTY OLD TOY.
*SEE THE "TOY STORY: THE RETURN OF BUZZ LIGHTYEAR" TRADE PAPERBACK FOR DETAILS! -AARON
GO!
RERR.
HEY... *HUFF* WAIT FOR M--
AH!
RUN FOR YOUR LIVES!!!
AHHHHHHHH!!!...
ARF ARF!!!...

STAMINA: THE JUMPING-JACK CHALLENGE!
AFTER 20 MINUTES.
AFTER 40.
Z Z
AFTER 50.
CLICK!
GASP! NEED... AIR!
AFTER 1 HOUR!
THIS... REALLY... ISN'T... FAIR--

SPECIAL TALENTS
HOWDY, HOWDY, HOWDY!!!

HI-YAH!

STILL HOLDING.
STILL HOLDING.

SMOOCH!

NO? YOU MEAN YOU WEREN'T SCARED AT ALL?
CAN I JUST TRY ONE MORE TIME?

DOES THIS COUNT?

ROPE TRICKS: LASSO!
LET'S SEE SOMEONE ROPE BETTER THAN THI--OH *COME ON!*
HEH.
UH... I GOT 'IM!
UM...A LITTLE HELP HERE?
WHAT IS YOUR MAJOR MALFUNCTION?!
HEY!

FLIGHT: FALLING WITH STYLE!
SPRING!

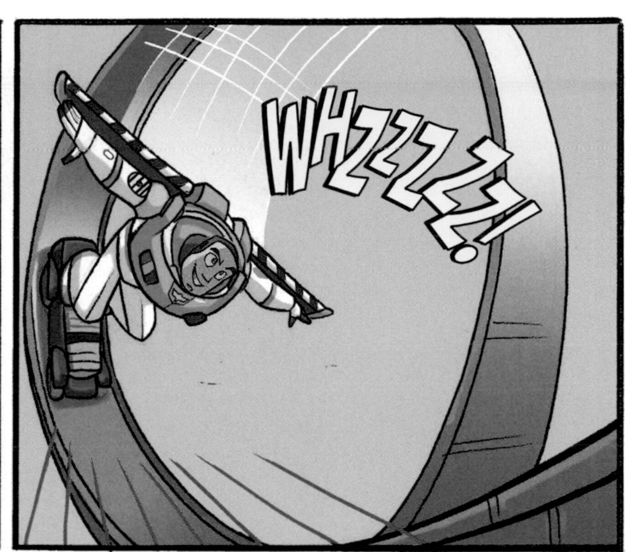
WHZZZZZ!

TO INFINITY...AND BEYOND!

ANDY
BZZZZZZZZZ

HA!
SHOWOFF.

WHO'S NEXT?
NOBODY? NOBODY ELSE?
WELL... I GUESS I'LL GO...

I HAVE A *BAD* FEELING ABOUT THIS...

C'MON, WOODY...WE DON'T HAVE ALL DAY!

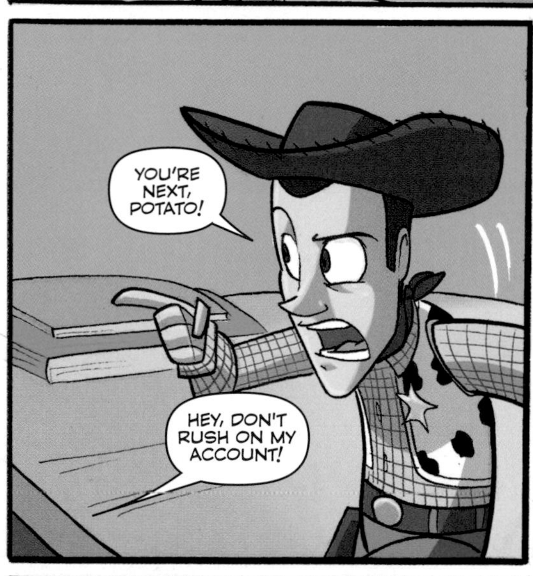
YOU'RE NEXT, POTATO!
HEY, DON'T RUSH ON MY ACCOUNT!

WHOA, WHOA WHOA...!

I'M GONNA DIE!

WAAAH!!

AH!

NWHHHHHHOO

OOOAAAA

SNAP!!!

HE'S DOOMED!
THAT AIN'T GOOD!
THE WINDOW, WOODY! WATCH THE *WINDOW!*

AAAARRRGGH!!

AAAHHHHHH!

CHAPTER TWO
AAAHHHHHH!

AAAHHHHHH!
HE'S FLYING!
THAT AIN'T FLYING, IT'S...FALLING *WITHOUT* STYLE!

WELL, IF I KNOW WOODY, HE'LL PULL IT OUT AT THE LAST POSSIBLE SECOND.

THUNK!

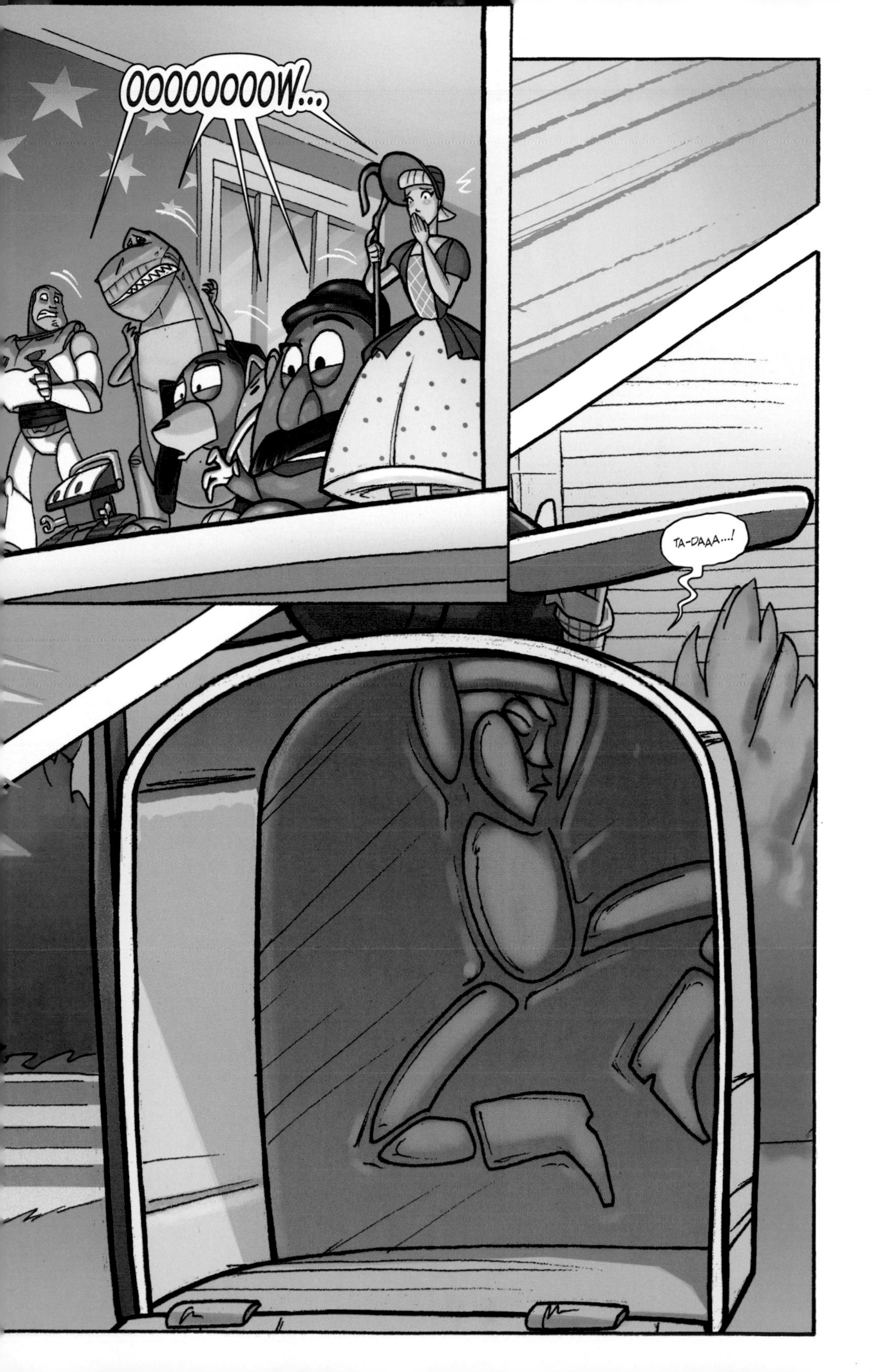
OOOOOOOOOW...
TA-DAAA...!

AN HOUR LATER...
WHO'S NEXT?

FLYING: FALLING WITH STYLE COMPETITION (CONTINUED)
001!!!

YIPPI-KI-YAY!

YOU COWARD!

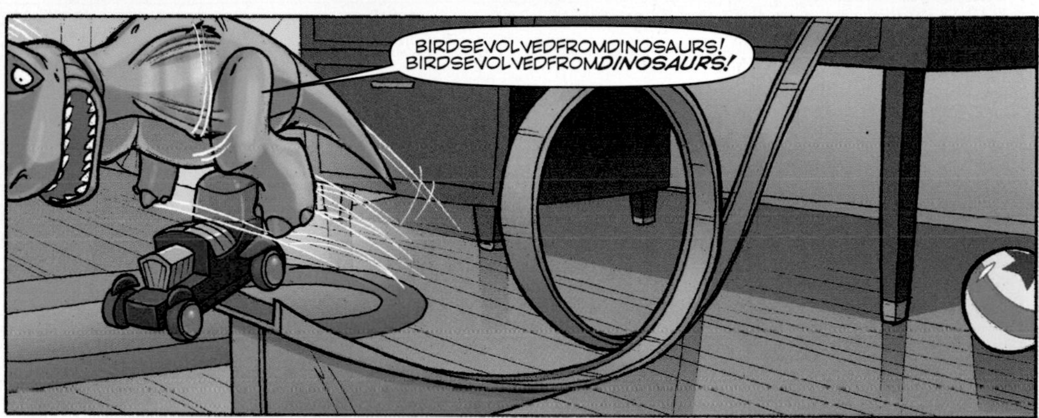
BIRDSEVOLVEDFROMDINOSAURS!
BIRDSEVOLVEDFROMDINOSAURS!

WHEN PIGS FL--!

NO! SOMEBODY LEFT THE WINDOW OPEN AGAAAAAAAAAAAA--

AAAH!
ARF!

HEY! I'M WOODY! "AAAHHHHHHHH!"

WHAT ARE YOU LOOKING AT?

SCORES
JUDGES

SCORES

A "2"?!
I DON'T WANT YOUR PITY!

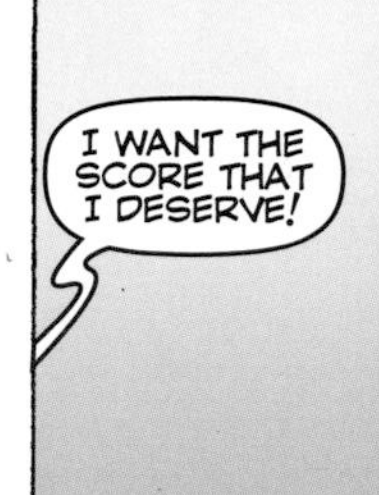
I WANT THE SCORE THAT I DESERVE!

ETCH!
OH, HARDY HAR *HAR*.

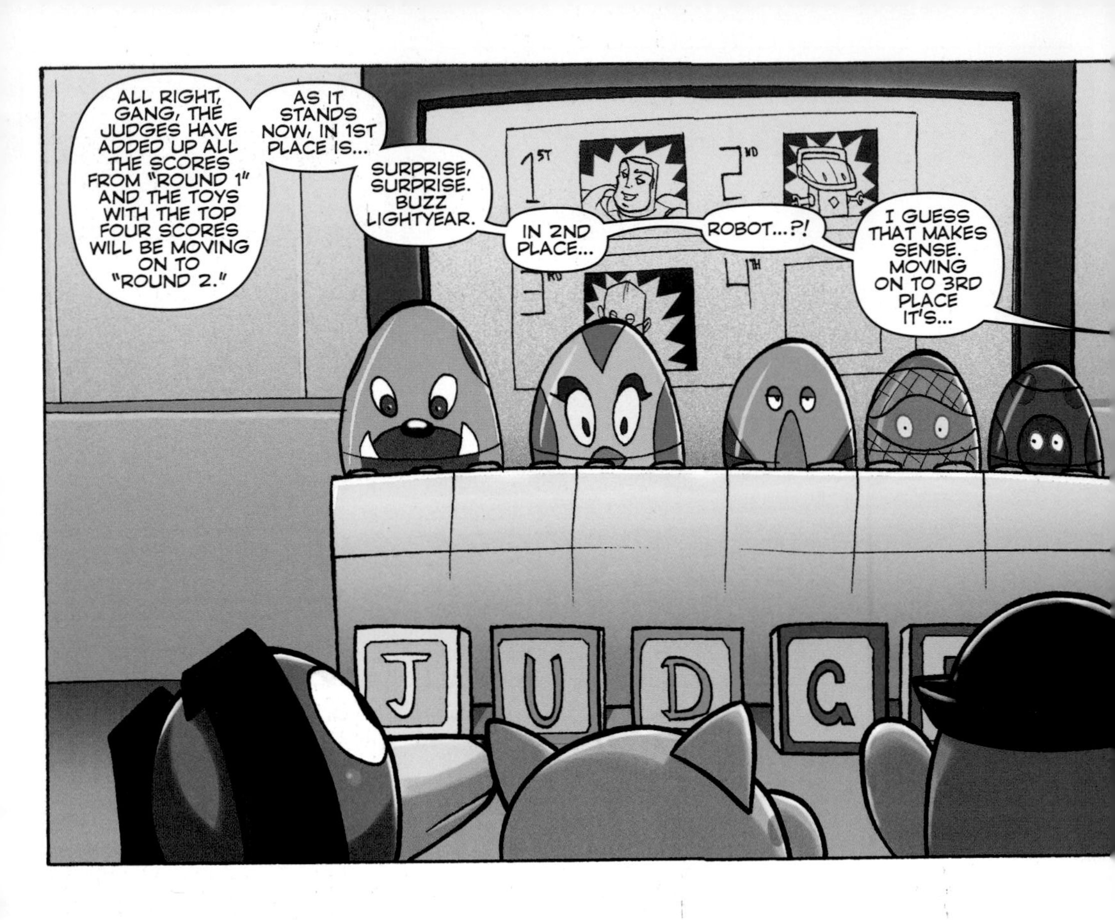
ALL RIGHT, GANG, THE JUDGES HAVE ADDED UP ALL THE SCORES FROM "ROUND 1" AND THE TOYS WITH THE TOP FOUR SCORES WILL BE MOVING ON TO "ROUND 2."
AS IT STANDS NOW, IN 1ST PLACE IS...
SURPRISE, SURPRISE. BUZZ LIGHTYEAR.
IN 2ND PLACE...
ROBOT...?!
I GUESS THAT MAKES SENSE. MOVING ON TO 3RD PLACE IT'S...
1ST
2ND
3RD
4TH
JUDG

AND IN 4TH PLACE IT'S...
4TH
REX.
IT IS?!
IT IS?
IT IS.

ROCKY?! OH, COME ON! SERIOUSLY?
AND IN 4TH PLACE WE HAVE...
...

OH, COME ON ETCH, DON'T MAKE US WAIT!

CONGRATULATIONS, BUDDY.
WAIT, LOOK...!

IT'S A "TIE!"
IT'S REX AND WOODY IN 4TH PLACE!
A TIE? OH, THANK YOU...
YOU KNOW WOODY; YOU CAN STILL CALL THIS WHOLE THING OFF.
I TOLD YOU WHAT'S GOING TO HAPPEN IF YOU DON'T WIN.
YOU DON'T THINK I CAN WIN.
THAT'S NOT WHAT THIS IS ABOUT, WOODY.
THAT'S NOT WHAT THIS IS ABOUT? I'LL TELL YOU WHAT THIS IS ABOUT...
THIS IS ABOUT YEARS OF "WOODY THE COWBOY" SAVING THE DAY, BECAUSE ANDY THOUGHT I SHOULD.
NO... BECAUSE ANDY THOUGHT I COULD.
AND MAYBE I CAN'T. MAYBE I'M NOT THE ACTION HERO THAT HE THINKS I AM.
YOU CERTAINLY DON'T THINK SO AND NEITHER DO THEY. HECK...MAYBE EVEN I DON'T BELIEVE IT...
...BUT THAT DOESN'T MEAN I'M GONNA GIVE UP.
'CAUSE ANDY BELIEVES IN ME...AND I CAN'T LET HIM DOWN.
ANDY

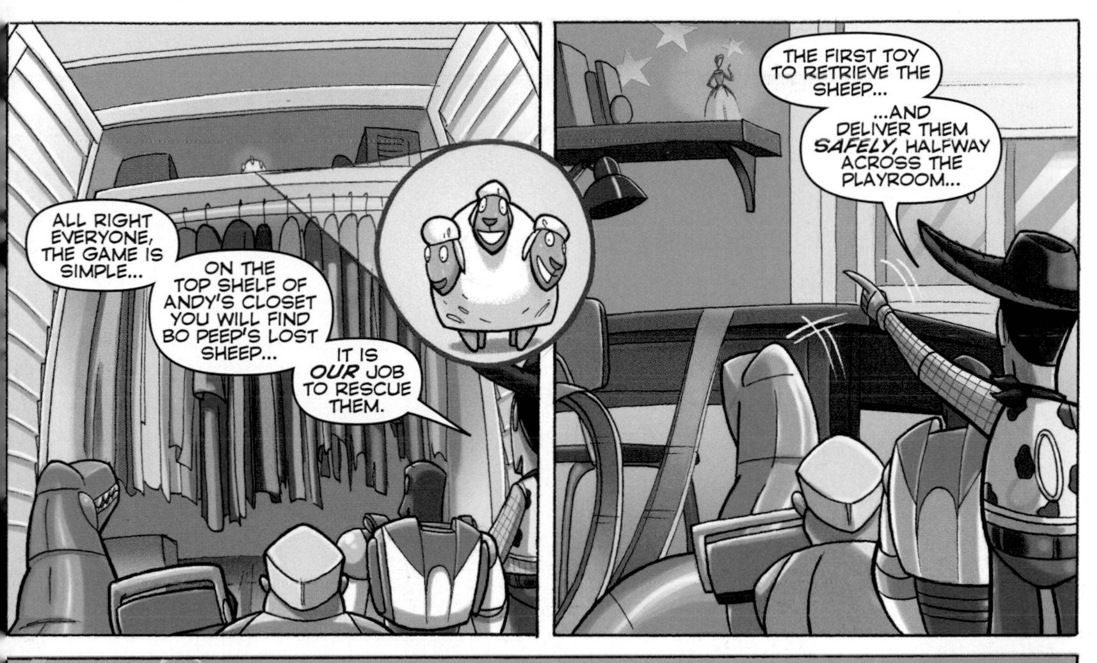
ALL RIGHT EVERYONE, THE GAME IS SIMPLE...
ON THE TOP SHELF OF ANDY'S CLOSET YOU WILL FIND BO PEEP'S LOST SHEEP...
IT IS *OUR* JOB TO RESCUE THEM.
THE FIRST TOY TO RETRIEVE THE SHEEP...
...AND DELIVER THEM *SAFELY,* HALFWAY ACROSS THE PLAYROOM...

...TO THE TENDER CARE OF *BO PEEP,* IS THE WINNER.
AND THE WINNER GETS THE GREATEST PRIZE I CAN THINK OF...
...A *KISS.*
PLAY NICE, BOYS.
WHAT ARE THE RULES?
NO RULES. EVERY TOY FOR HIMSELF.
NO RULES?! BUT WHAT WILL I HIDE BEHIND?!
NO RULES IS *GOOD* RULES.
COMPETITORS ON YOUR MARKS...
GET SET...
...*GO!*

THIS IS NOT A FAIR CONTEST!
I CAN'T REACH EITHER, REX. QUIT COMPLAINING AND THINK CONSTRUCTIVELY.

BUT THIS IS RIDICULOUS; I CAN'T CLIMB UP THERE! I CAN'T EVEN DO A PULL UP!

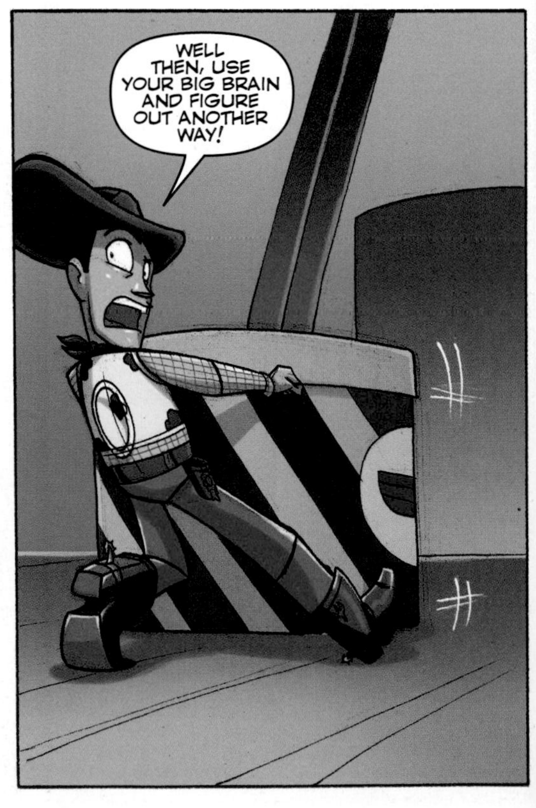
WELL THEN, USE YOUR BIG BRAIN AND FIGURE OUT ANOTHER WAY!

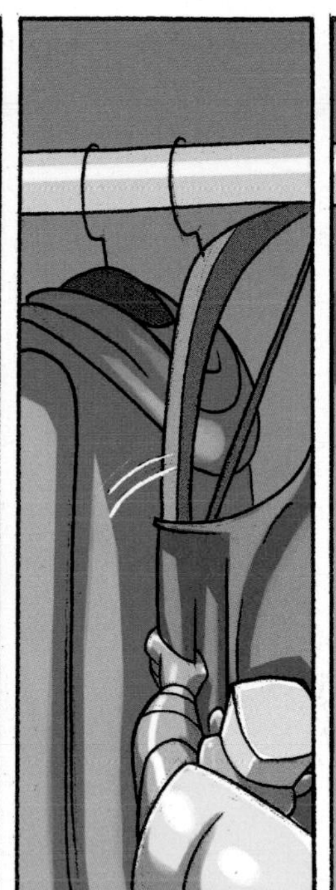

!

KEEP TRYING REX, YOU'LL GET IT. WHOA, WATCH OUT!
ANDY

I'M TELLING YOU, I CAN'T REACH--!
BAM!
HE *FELL?* I DIDN'T EVEN THINK ABOUT *FALLING!*
I DON'T THINK I CAN DO THIS.

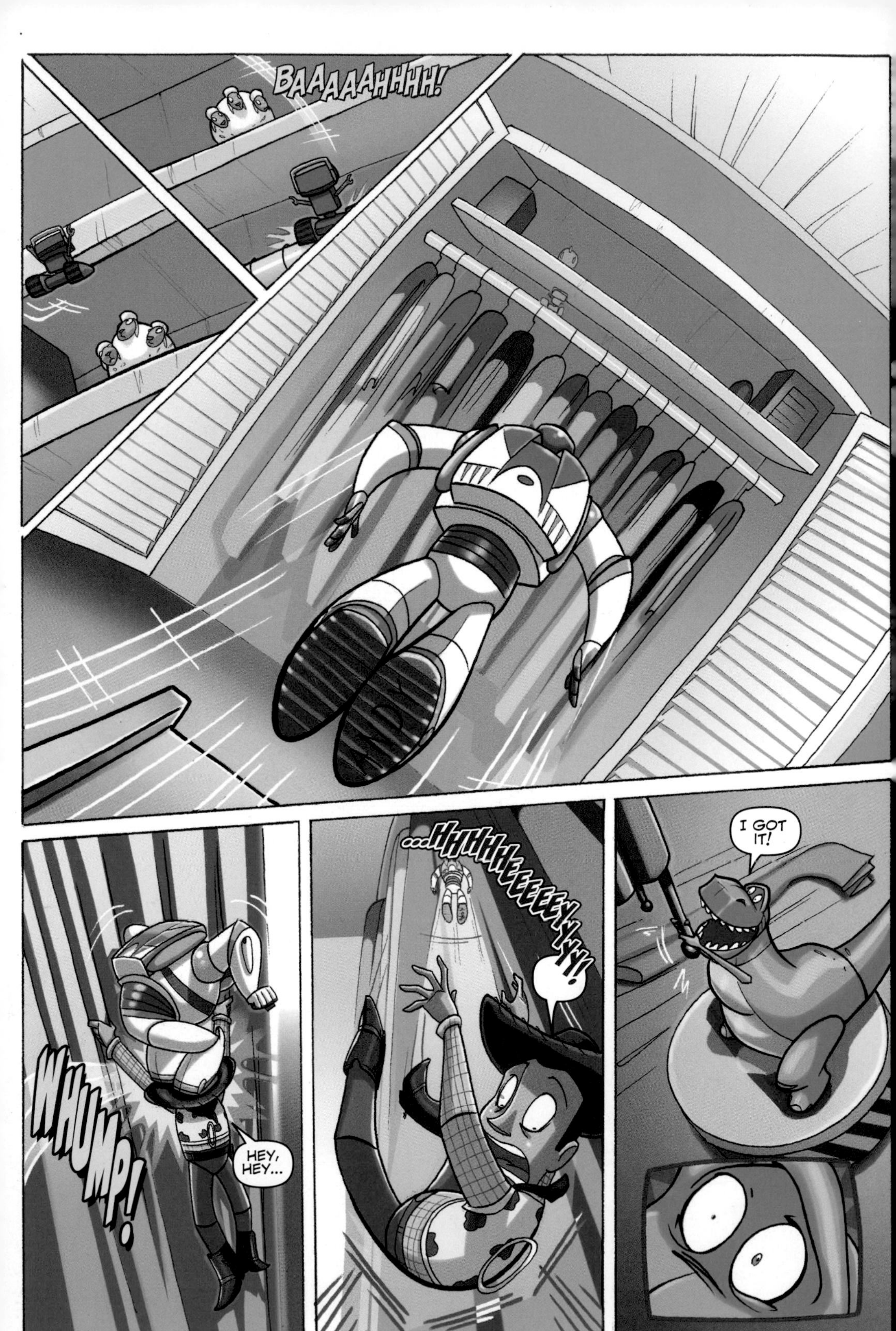
BAAAAAHHHH!
WHUMP!
HEY, HEY...
...HHHHHEEEEEYYYY!
I GOT IT!

CRASH!
CLANG!
CLICK!
BAAAAAHHHH!

THAP!

OH, NO!
BAH...?!

BAAAAAHHHH!
I GOTCHA, I GOTCHA!
CATCH!
WHOOSH
SLAM!
ANDY
COME ON WOODY... WE CAN SHARE 'EM!

DANK OW!
YOINK!

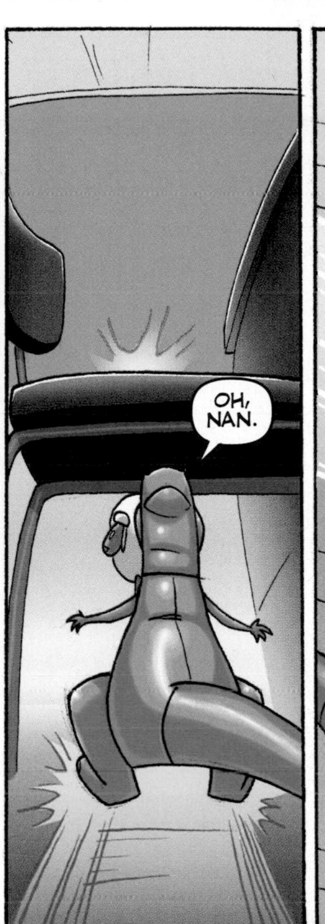
OH, NAN.

SLAM!

YOINK!

Ø11Ø?!!!

SWIPE!

OH, MY HEAD...
OH, NO, YOU DON'T...!

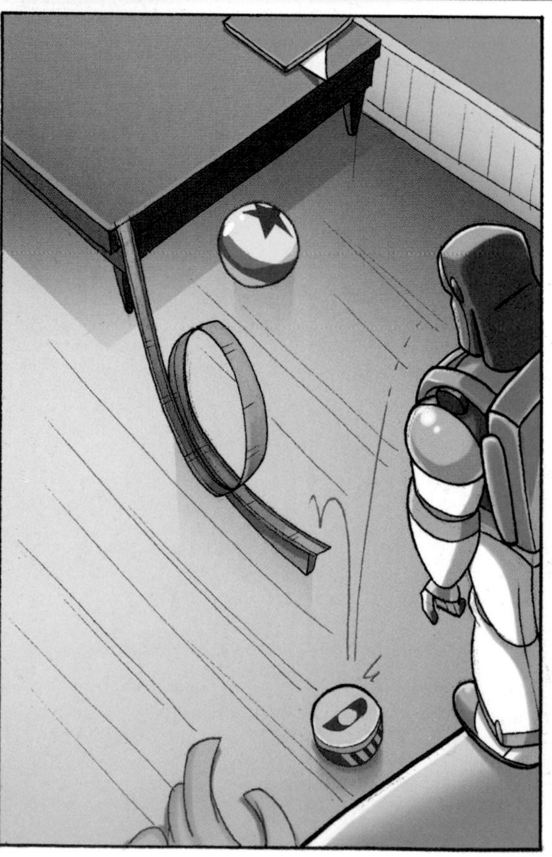

TO INFINITY... AND BEYOND!

SPRING!
BOUNCE!
I'VE GOTTA...WIN IT...FOR... ANDY!

YOINK!

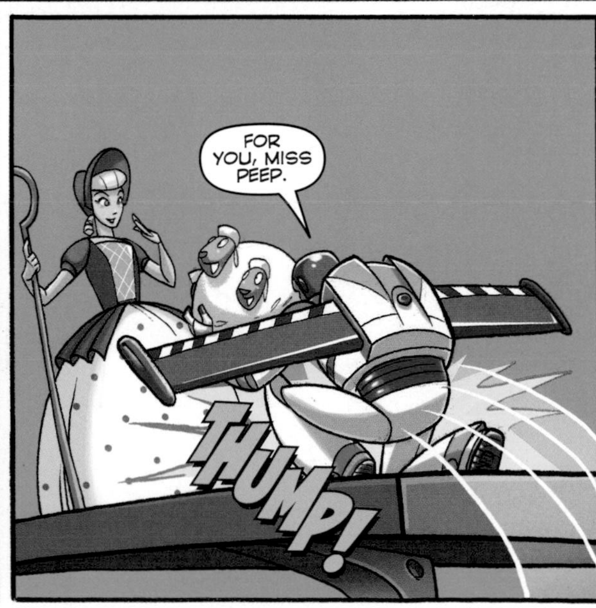
FOR YOU, MISS PEEP.
THUMP!

SMOOCH!

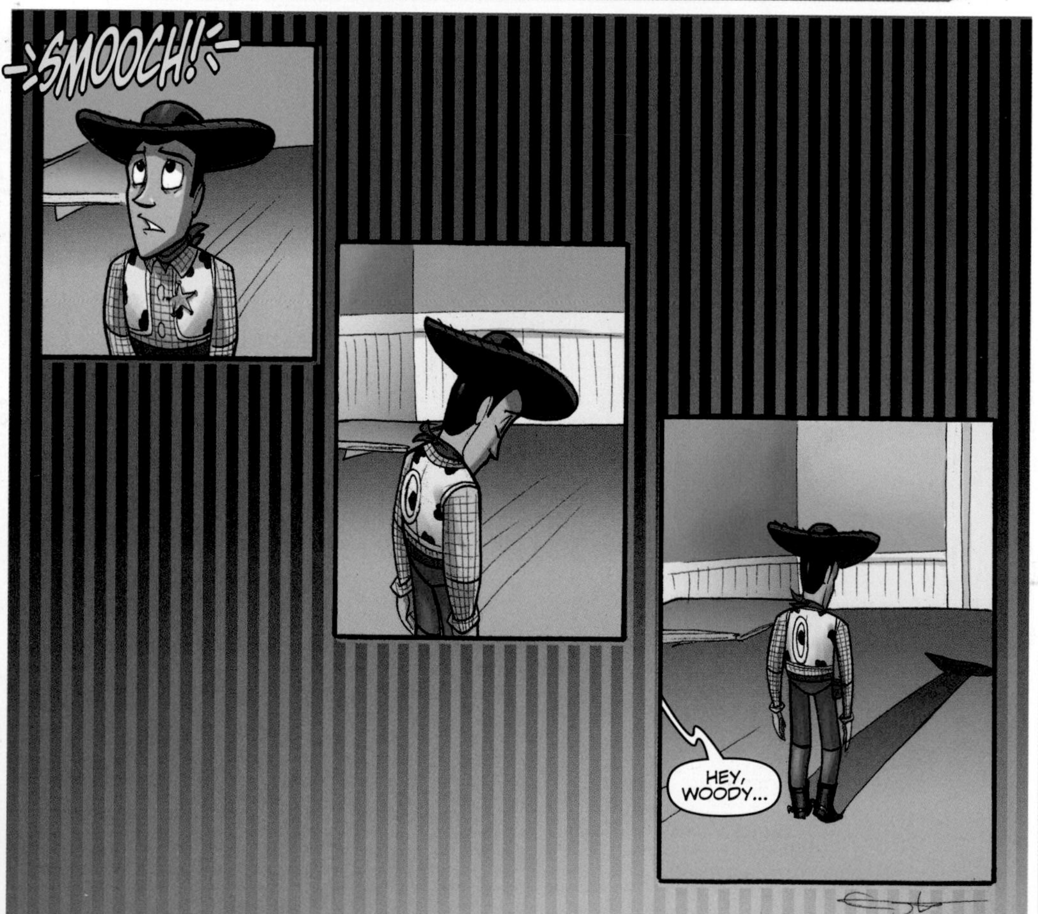
SMOOCH!
HEY, WOODY...

KIIIIISSSSSSSSSS!
BUT... BUT I LOST...
WOODY, YOU'VE ALWAYS GOTTEN YOUR KISSES FOR FREE.
I DON'T LOVE YOU BECAUSE YOU SAVE MY SHEEP.
I JUST LOVE YOU.
AND NOBODY CAN EVER CHANGE THAT.
I'M SORRY ABOUT...
IT'S ALL RIGHT, I UNDERSTAND... BUT DON'T YOU EVER DO ANYTHING LIKE THAT AGAIN.
YES, MA'AM.
THAT'S WHAT I LIKE TO HEAR. YOU KNOW...
...BUZZ SAID HE'D WATCH THE SHEEP TONIGHT.

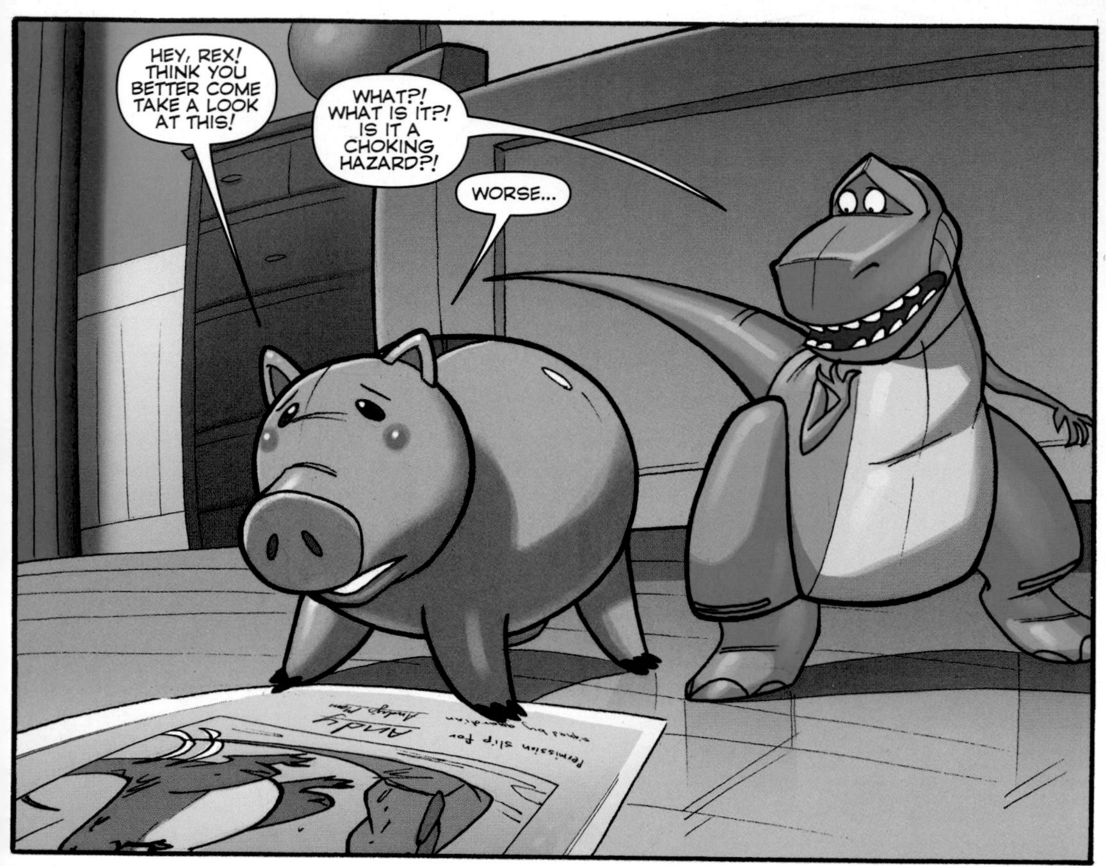
HEY, REX! THINK YOU BETTER COME TAKE A LOOK AT THIS!
WHAT?! WHAT IS IT?! IS IT A CHOKING HAZARD?!
WORSE...

...IT'S A FIELD TRIP!
Permission slip for Andy
signed by guardian Andy's Mom
A FIELD TRIP? TO A DINOSAUR MUSEUM...?!
BUT...BUT ANDY...BOUGHT ME FROM A MUSEUM GIFT SHOP...

NOOOOOOOOOOOOOOOOO!
IS REX BEING REPLACED? CAN HE STOP ANDY FROM BUYING ANOTHER DINOSAUR?
FIND OUT NEXT TIME IN ANOTHER THRILLING INSTALLMENT OF TOY STORY!

CHAPTER THREE
These new toys are sooo much better than my old ones!
DINO MUSEUM
DINO MUSEUM
I never knew how many awesome dinosaurs there were!
Andy... dinner!!!
Awww...I just finished opening 'em!

Um...is, is, is anybody up there...?
NO...!

WE'RE DOWN HERE...
...AND WE'RE HUNGRY!

AAAARRRRGGGHHHHHH!!!

WHAM!
Who, who...who are you?!
I'M YOUR REPLACEMENT!!!

ANDY DOESN'T NEED YOU ANYMORE!!!

No! Please! I can be scary! Just give me another chance!

NO!!!
WHERE'S ANDY?!
HE'S IN THE BATHROOM GETTING READY FOR SCHOOL. ARE YOU ALL RIGHT?
NO, I'M NOT ALL RIGHT! ANDY IS GOING TO THE DINOSAUR MUSEUM AND HE'S GONNA BUY A NEW DINOSAUR TOY!

CALM DOWN, REX. IF ANDY WAS GONNA BUY ANYTHING, HAMM WOULD KNOW ABOUT IT.

HAMM, HAS ANDY MADE ANY WITHDRAWALS RECENTLY?
NO SIR, ONLY DEPOSITS.

SEE?
MOM, CAN I HAVE SOME MONEY FOR THE DINOSAUR MUSEUM GIFT SHOP?
SURE SWEETIE, HOW ABOUT... $25?
GREAT! THANKS, MOM!

AH! WHAT ARE WE GONNA DO?! WHAT ARE WE GONNA DO?! WE'VE GOTTA DO SOME--!!!
PULL YOURSELF TOGETHER, MAN!
SMACK!
OW!!!
ANDY'S GONNA REPLACE ME WITH A NEWER, SCARIER DINOSAUR, AND NOW MY FACE HURTS AND I'M DIZZY!
ANDY IS NOT GOING TO REPLACE YOU.
THAT'S RIGHT HE'S NOT!
BECAUSE WE'RE GONNA GO TO THAT MUSEUM OURSELVES AND MAKE SURE HE DOESN'T.
WE ARE?
WE ARE?!
YES, WE ARE. AND HERE'S HOW WE'RE GONNA DO IT...
WHISPER, WHISPER, WHISPER...
CAN YOU BELIEVE THOSE GUYS? PLOTTING AN ADVENTURE WITHOUT INCLUDING US!
THE NERVE.
DON'T YOU WORRY HAMM; I'VE GOT A PLAN THAT'LL TIE US DIRECTLY INTO THE ACTION!

TWENTY-FIVE BUCKS!
I'M GONNA GET YOU GUYS A NEW FRIEND!

C'MON HONEY, YOU'RE GONNA MISS YOUR FIELD TRIP!
HUH. FEELS HEAVY...
...I GOTTA RETURN ALL THOSE LIBRARY BOOKS.
DEEP SPACE
WILD WEST

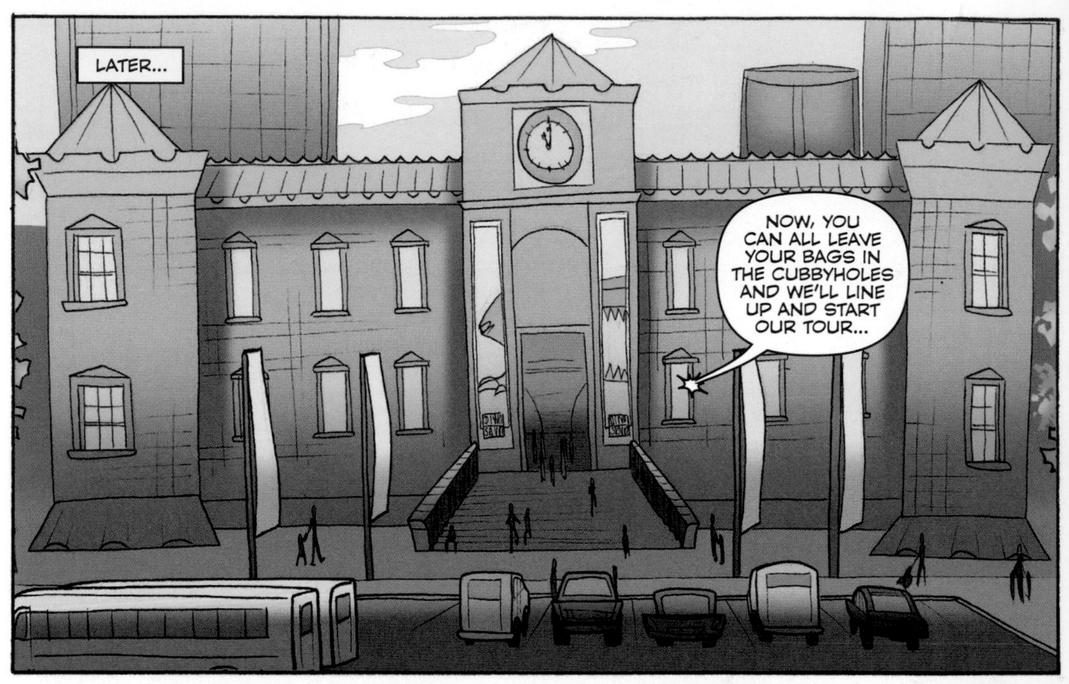
LATER...
NOW, YOU CAN ALL LEAVE YOUR BAGS IN THE CUBBYHOLES AND WE'LL LINE UP AND START OUR TOUR...

DINO SAUR
I CAN'T WAIT 'TIL THE GIFT SHOP AT THE END; I'M GONNA BUY A NEW DINOSAUR!
COOL!

A B C D E F G H
Jurassic is Fantastic

PLOP!

ZIP!

ALL RIGHT, TOYS...LET'S MOVE OUT!

WELL, YOU HEARD THE TOY! LET'S MOVE OUT!

HUT! HUT! HUT! HUT! HUT! HUT!

GET YOUR STINKIN' PAWS IN GEAR, YA DIRTY APES!
OOH-OOH-EEE-HEE!

HEY! WAIT FOR ME!!!
LIGHTYEAR, I BELIEVE WE HAVE A STOW-AWAY!

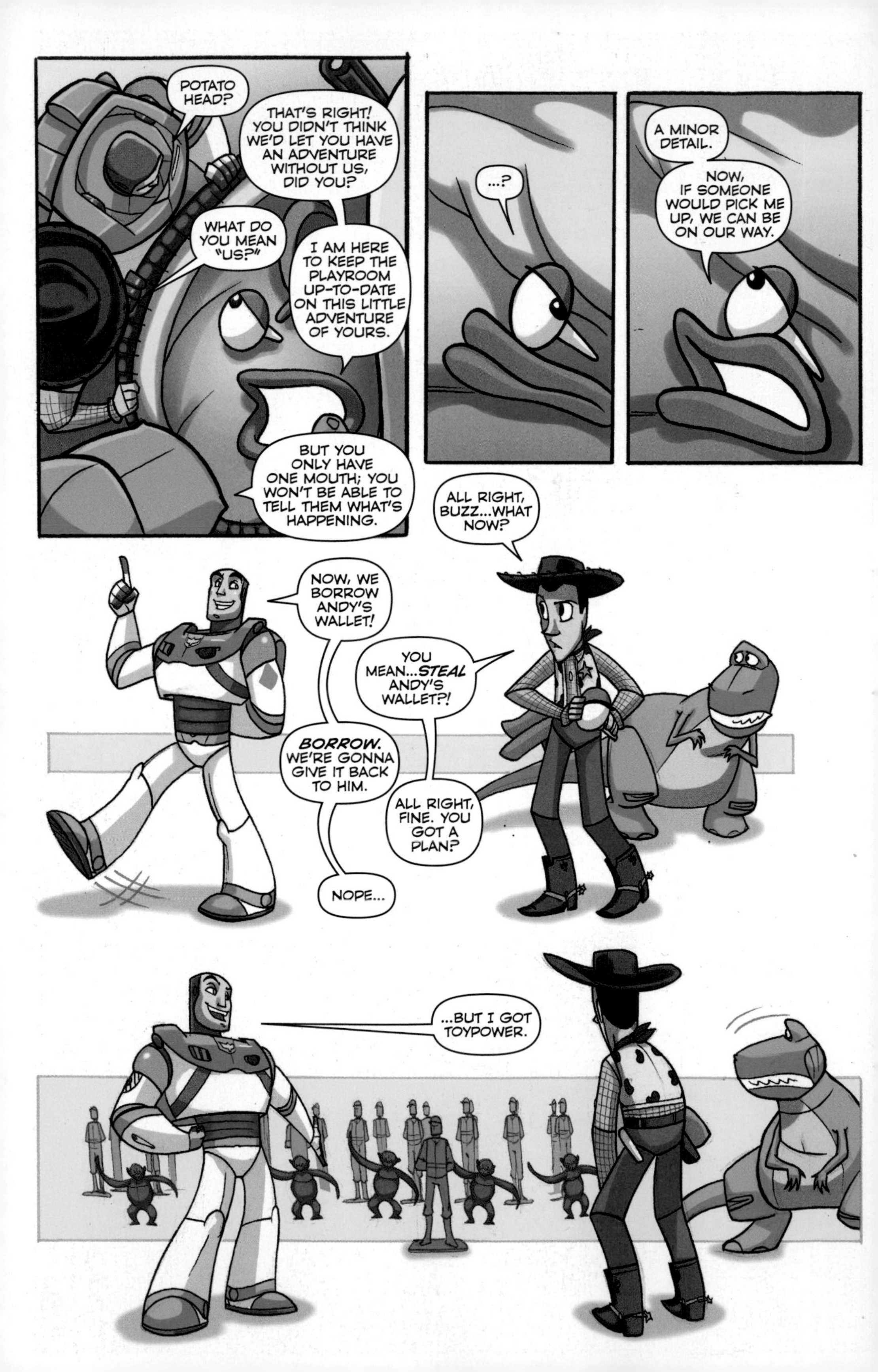
POTATO HEAD?
THAT'S RIGHT! YOU DIDN'T THINK WE'D LET YOU HAVE AN ADVENTURE WITHOUT US, DID YOU?
WHAT DO YOU MEAN "US?"
I AM HERE TO KEEP THE PLAYROOM UP-TO-DATE ON THIS LITTLE ADVENTURE OF YOURS.
BUT YOU ONLY HAVE ONE MOUTH; YOU WON'T BE ABLE TO TELL THEM WHAT'S HAPPENING.
...?
A MINOR DETAIL.
NOW, IF SOMEONE WOULD PICK ME UP, WE CAN BE ON OUR WAY.
ALL RIGHT, BUZZ...WHAT NOW?
NOW, WE BORROW ANDY'S WALLET!
YOU MEAN...*STEAL* ANDY'S WALLET?!
BORROW. WE'RE GONNA GIVE IT BACK TO HIM.
ALL RIGHT, FINE. YOU GOT A PLAN?
NOPE...
...BUT I GOT TOYPOWER.

SO...WHAT WHEEZE NOW?
NOTHING. GENIUS HERE FORGOT THAT HE'S ONLY GOT ONE MOUTH!
MAYBE MRS. POTATO HEAD HAS A SPARE!
NOPE.
OH, YES YOU DO.
POP!
WELL, THAT'S BETTER!
HA, HA, HA!
YOU SOUND LIKE A GIRLY TOY!
WHAT'S THAT SUPPOSED MEAN?!
UM... NOTHING. JUST THAT...
YOU'RE RIGHT, IT MEANS NOTHING. NOW, KEEP YOUR TRAP SHUT OR THIS "GIRLY TOY" IS GONNA TOSS YOU RIGHT OUT THE WINDOW!
SO, WHAT'S GOING ON AT THE MUSEUM?
I'M NOT SURE.
WELL, WHAT ARE THEY SAYING?
YEAH, THAT'S THE THING...WOODY LEFT MY EAR IN THE BACKPACK.

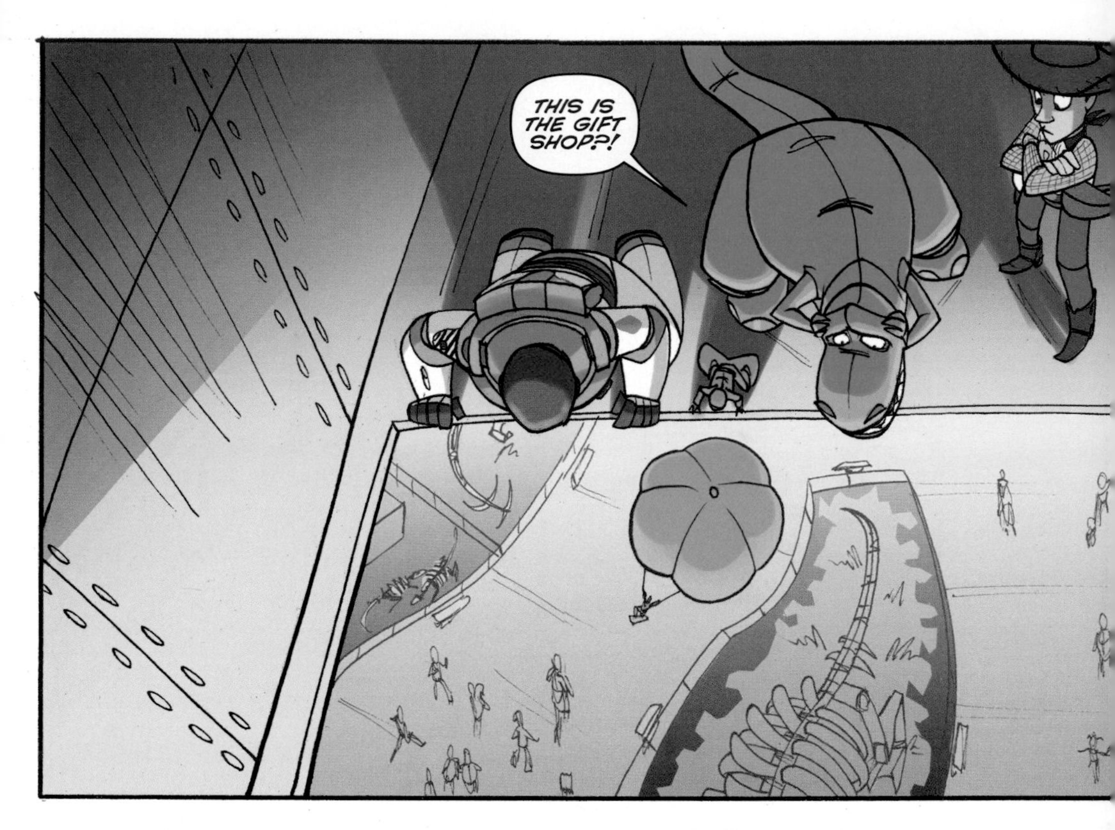
THIS IS THE GIFT SHOP?!

STOP SAYING THAT, POTATO!
WHAT? I'M SORRY... DID YOU SAY SOMETHING? I COULDN'T HEAR YOU, BECAUSE SOMEONE FORGOT TO BRING MY EAR!
I SAID I WAS SORRY.
TOO BAD I CAN'T READ LIPS...THAT LOOKED LIKE A SINCERE APOLOGY.

SO...HOW YOU LIKING THE GIFT SHOP, REX?
I HATE THE GIFT SHOP!
WILL YOU STOP LISTENING TO HIM?! THIS IS NOT THE GIFT SHOP, ALL RIGHT?! THIS IS THE MUSEUM! ANDY COULDN'T BUY ANY OF THIS STUFF IF HE WANTED TO.

NO, NO, NO, THIS IS *NOT* THE GIFT SHOP!
YEAH, THAT'S THE GIFT SHOP, ALL RIGHT.
I'M SO CONFUSED!

NOW, WILL YOU CALM DOWN; EVERYTHING IS GOING TO BE FINE.
YOU PROMISE?
...
IF IT'LL MAKE YOU FEEL BETTER, SURE... I PROMISE.
OH, THANK YOU WOODY! THANK YOU SO MUCH!
HEY, WATCH OUT! YOU'RE MAKING MY EYE POP OUT OF ITS HOLSTER!

HOPE YOU TOYS HAVE SOME GOOD NEWS, BECAUSE I JUST PROMISED REX THAT EVERYTHING WAS GOING TO BE OKAY.
WAIT FOR IT...
BULLSEYE!
KNEW THAT BOY'D DO THE RIGHT THING, I AIN'T EVER SEEN HIM LEAVE A MAN BEHIND.
THAT BOY IS STANDING DIRECTLY UNDER OUR DROP ZONE, BOYS, JUST WHERE WE WANTED HIM.
NOW IT'S TIME FOR OPERATION: COWBOY DANGLE.
OPERATION WHAT?!

THIS IS A TERRIBLE PLAN!
THIS IS A TERRIBLE PLAN.
THIS SPINOSAURUS FOSSIL DISCOVERY IN 2005 WAS ESTIMATED TO BE 52-59 FEET LONG, MAKING IT THE BIGGEST THEROPOD DINOSAUR THAT EVER LIVED-*EVEN BIGGER THAN THE TYRANNOSAURUS REX!*
WOW, COOL!
HEY, IT'S ANDY!
SHUT UP!
YOU SAY SOMETHING?

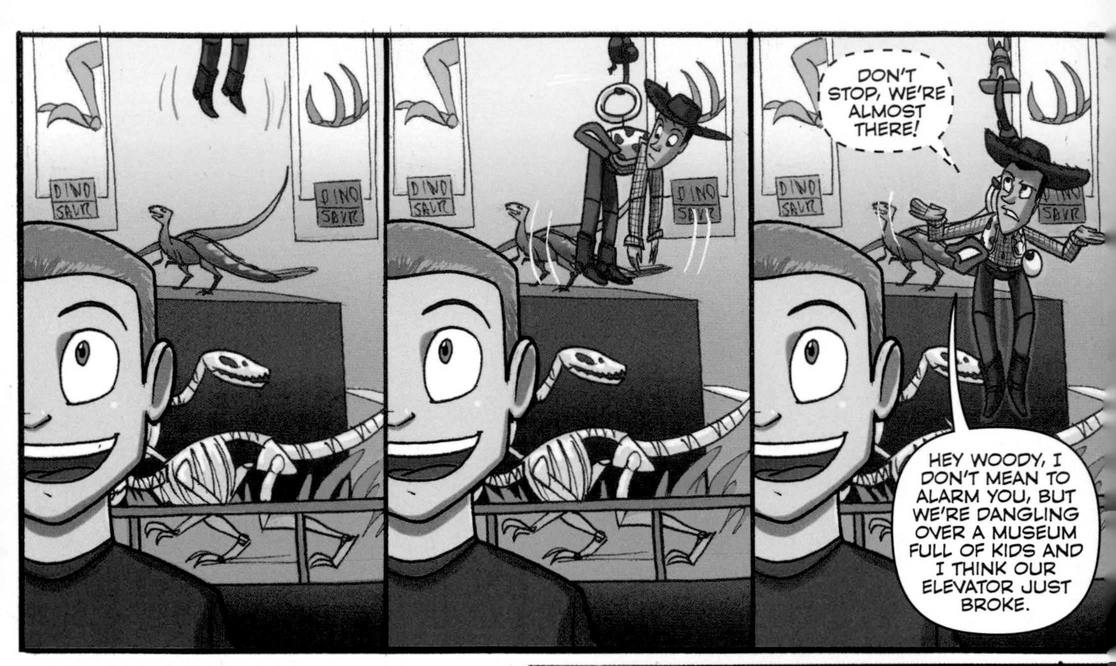
DINO SAUR
DINO SAUR
DON'T STOP, WE'RE ALMOST THERE!
HEY WOODY, I DON'T MEAN TO ALARM YOU, BUT WE'RE DANGLING OVER A MUSEUM FULL OF KIDS AND I THINK OUR ELEVATOR JUST BROKE.

SARGE, WE NEED MORE ROPE HERE, WHAT'S THE HOLD UP?
WE'RE FRESH OUTTA MONKEYS, SOLDIER!

YOU'RE GONNA HAVE TO IMPROVISE, WE'RE OUTTA MONKEYS!
GREAT...
WAIT, DON'T TELL ME...THEY RAN OUTTA MONKEYS?

SO, NOW WE'RE JUST HANGING THERE!
I WANNA SEE THE TOUR GUIDE EXPLAIN THAT ATTRACTION! "AND OVER HERE, THE DANGLING COWBOY-A-SAURUS..."
OH, NO!
I TOLD 'EM THEY SHOULDA EMPTIED THE BARREL!
OOH-OOH-EH!
WAIT, I THINK WOODY'S GOT A PLAN!
PLEASE, BE LONG ENOUGH. PLEASE, BE LONG ENOUGH.
NO, WAIT--!
OH, THIS IS RIDICULOUS! HEY, MONKEY, JUST LET HIM GO!

WHIP!
YOU'RE MY FAVORITE DEPUTY!!!
WOODY...?
QUICK! PULL UP!

ANDY, COME ON KIDDO, THE TOUR IS MOVING ON!
BUT...I COULDA SWORN I...

WHAT?
NEVER MIND...MUST HAVE BEEN MY IMAGINATION.
WHOOPS.
WHOOPS?
WOODY! DID WE GET IT?!
WELL DONE, EVERYONE! WE GOT IT!
THANK YOU, *HUF* THANK YOU, *PUFF* THANK YOU...
FINISH YOUR NAPS AND THEN WE'RE HEADING BACK TO BASE...
...OUR JOB HERE IS DONE!

IT'S EMPTY!!!

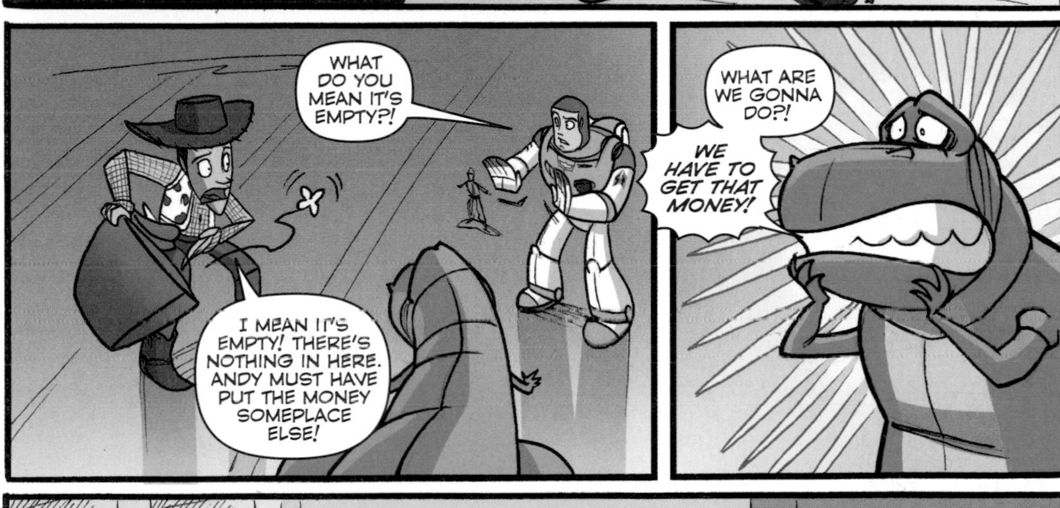
WHAT DO YOU MEAN IT'S EMPTY?!
I MEAN IT'S EMPTY! THERE'S NOTHING IN HERE. ANDY MUST HAVE PUT THE MONEY SOMEPLACE ELSE!
WHAT ARE WE GONNA DO?!
WE HAVE TO GET THAT MONEY!

THE FIELD TRIP'S OVER IN 10 MINUTES. THEY'RE PROBABLY IN THE GIFT SHOP RIGHT NOW!!!
DON'T LOOK AT ME! THERE'S NO TIME TO GET IT!
I'M A GONER!!!
IT'S OKAY, YOU'RE GONNA BE FINE!
NO, I'M NOT! HE'S GONNA GET ONE OF THOSE SPINOSAURUS DINOSAURS AND IT'S GONNA EAT ME!

SEE? I TOLD REX HE HAD NOTHING TO WORRY ABOUT.
SHOULD I TELL 'EM YOU TOOK THE MONEY BEFORE ANDY LEFT THIS MORNING?
WHAT FUN WOULD THAT BE?
DON'T YOU JUST LOVE A HAPPY ENDING...?

CHAPTER FOUR
THERE! A CAMPFIRE, JUST LIKE AT COWBOY CAMP!
YOU GLOW-BUGS OKAY IN THERE? COMFORTABLE?
YUP! THANKS, WOODY!
HEY, GATHER 'ROUND EVERYBODY! CAMP'S ALL SET UP!

YOU'VE DONE A FINE JOB HERE, COWBOY.
WITH ANDY AWAY AT THAT SLEEPOVER, I THOUGHT WE'D HAVE A CAMPOUT OF OUR OWN!
THE FIRST THING WE DO AT CAMP IS SING SONGS AROUND THE FIRE.
MR. CRANK, IF YOU PLEASE.
OH, GIVE ME A HOME...
...WHERE THE DINOSAURS ROAM...

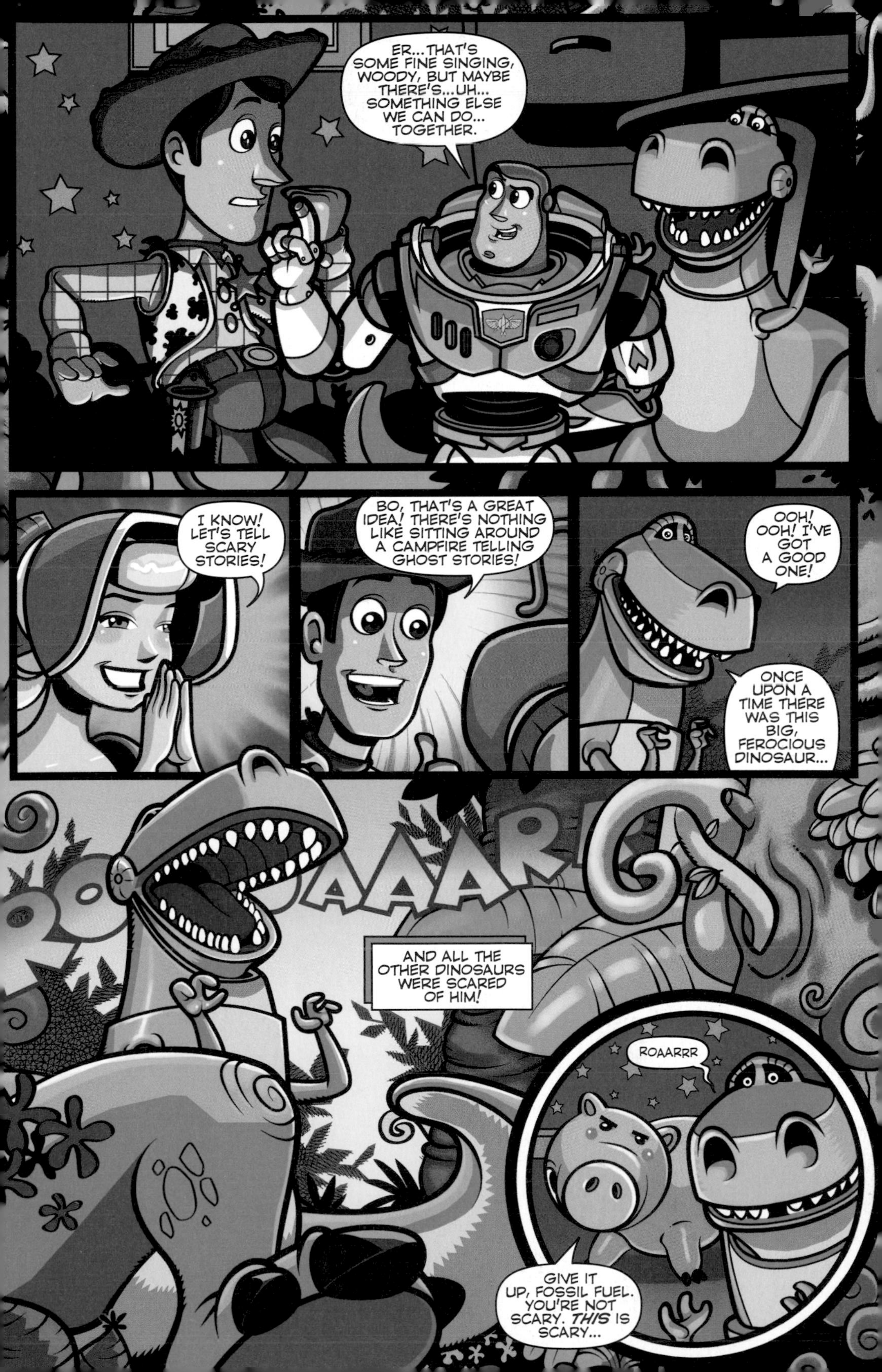

ER... THAT'S SOME FINE SINGING, WOODY, BUT MAYBE THERE'S...UH... SOMETHING ELSE WE CAN DO... TOGETHER.
I KNOW! LET'S TELL SCARY STORIES!
BO, THAT'S A GREAT IDEA! THERE'S NOTHING LIKE SITTING AROUND A CAMPFIRE TELLING GHOST STORIES!
OOH! OOH! I'VE GOT A GOOD ONE!
ONCE UPON A TIME THERE WAS THIS BIG, FEROCIOUS DINOSAUR...
AND ALL THE OTHER DINOSAURS WERE SCARED OF HIM!
ROAARRR
GIVE IT UP, FOSSIL FUEL. YOU'RE NOT SCARY. *THIS* IS SCARY...

THIS IS THE STORY OF MY COUSIN, PORKY.
A PIGGY BANK JUST LIKE ME, PORKY WAS MINDING HIS OWN BUSINESS, UNTIL ONE DAY...
...HIS OWNER NEEDED SOME CASH.
I, EH, GUESS YOU COULD SAY THE BANKING SYSTEM CRASHED.

HMMM...IT SEEMS THE LITTLE GIRL WAS ONLY INTERESTED IN COMMERCE. HARDLY THAT FRIGHTENING.
TELL THAT TO THE PIECES OF MY COUSIN!
ME! ME!
GO AHEAD, ROCKY. TELL YOUR STORY.
GRRRRRRRRR
EEP!
FASCINATING STORY, ROCKY. REMINDS ME OF THE TIME I WAS ON CETI ALPHOOINE...

IT WAS A DANGEROUS MISSION, BUT STAR COMMAND KNEW IT WAS THE ONLY CHANCE TO STOP THE EVIL EMPEROR ZURG!
ZURG HAD DEVELOPED A NEW WEAPON-- ONE OF UNIMAGINABLE DESTRUCTIVE POWER!
IT WAS ALL UP TO ME.
IT'S ALL UP TO ME!

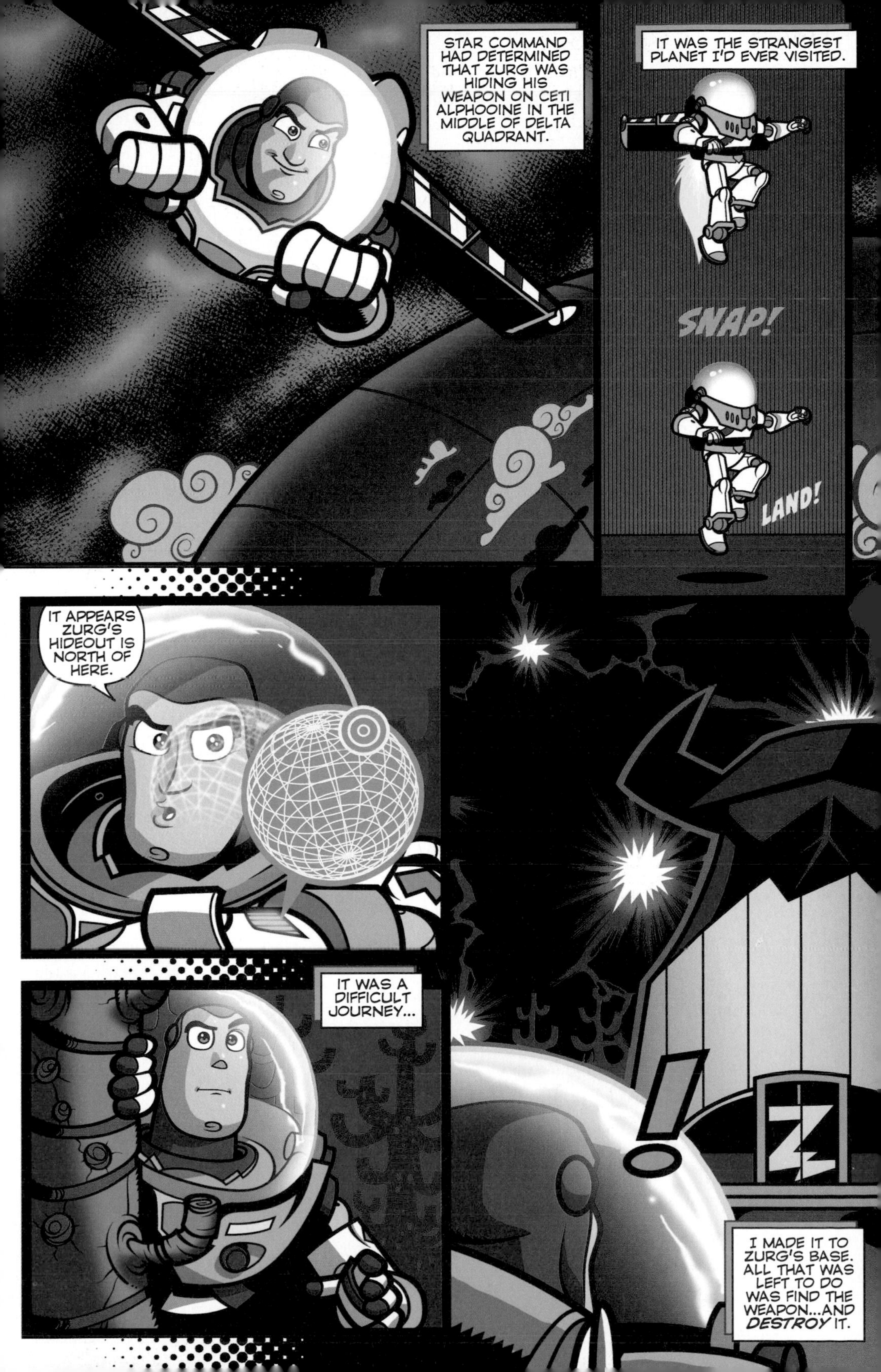
STAR COMMAND HAD DETERMINED THAT ZURG WAS HIDING HIS WEAPON ON CETI ALPHOOINE IN THE MIDDLE OF DELTA QUADRANT.
IT WAS THE STRANGEST PLANET I'D EVER VISITED.
SNAP!
LAND!
IT APPEARS ZURG'S HIDEOUT IS NORTH OF HERE.
IT WAS A DIFFICULT JOURNEY...
I MADE IT TO ZURG'S BASE. ALL THAT WAS LEFT TO DO WAS FIND THE WEAPON...AND *DESTROY* IT.

I KNEW THERE HAD TO BE A WAY IN.
BA-BOOM!!
I WAS GETTING CLOSE, I COULD FEEL IT.
I WAS SURE THE WEAPON WAS RIGHT BEHIND THAT DOOR.
I WENT TO OPEN IT...

IT WAS ZURG!
I'M SO GLAD YOU COULD JOIN ME.
ACK!
WHAT DID YOU DO?!
OBVIOUSLY, I ESCAPED FROM ZURG'S CLUTCHES.
AND DESTROYED THE WEAPON, SAVING THE GALAXY FROM CERTAIN DESTRUCTION.

THAT'S IT?! C'MON, BUZZ. THAT WASN'T A CAMPFIRE STORY!
IT WASN'T?
NO! CAMPFIRE STORIES ARE SUPPOSED TO SCARE YOU. THEY'RE SUPPOSED TO BE ABOUT GHOSTS OR MONSTERS OR... WELL, YOU KNOW.
WELL, IF YOU'RE SO GOOD AT IT, WOODY, WHY DON'T YOU TELL ONE?
ALL RIGHT, I WILL.
IT WAS A LONG TIME AGO, ON A NIGHT JUST LIKE TONIGHT...

ANDY TOOK ME WITH HIM TO COWBOY CAMP, LIKE HE DOES EVERY YEAR.
ANDY LEFT ME IN THE CABIN WHILE HE WENT OUT FOR A HOT DOG ROAST.
I...AHEM... FELL OFF THE BED. BUT I HEARD SOMETHING OUTSIDE. SOMETHING TERRIFYING!
WHOOOOOO
OF COURSE, I WASN'T AFRAID...SO I WENT TO HAVE A LOOK.
HELLLOOOOO?
WHOOOOOO
WHO'S OUT HERE?
WHOOOOOO

ANDY, WHERE ARE YOU WHEN I NEED YOU?
I'M NOT SCARED. I'M NOT SCARED. I'M NOT SCARED.
WHOOOOOO
WHOOOOOOO
AGGGGHHHHHH!
ANDY

I ALMOST THOUGHT IT WAS SCARY.
HEH, HEH. LAME.
OH, WOODY.
GUESS YOU HAD TO BE THERE.
YOU WANT SCARY? I'LL GIVE YOU SCARY.

YOU EVER HEAR OF THE ONE-ARMED TOY TAKER?
N-NO...
A FEW YEARS AGO, SOME KID'S TOYS STARTED DISAPPEARING.
SOMEONE...OR *SOMETHING*... WAS TAKING THEM AWAY.
THE KID THOUGHT SHE'D LOST HER FAVORITE TOYS.
BUT IT WAS WORSE...*MUCH* WORSE!

AT FIRST IT LOOKED LIKE IT WAS AN ISOLATED INCIDENT...JUST ONE KID'S TOYS. BUT THEN...ANOTHER KID'S TOYS DISAPPEARED!
EVEN TOUGH TOYS LIKE COMBAT CARL WEREN'T SAFE FROM THE TERRIBLE, ONE-ARMED MENACE!
POW!
EVERYONE IN THE TOY COMMUNITY WAS TERRIFIED!
WERE THE TOYS DISAPPEARING ON PURPOSE?
WHERE'S MY COMBAT CARL?
OR WAS IT SOMETHING FAR MORE *SINISTER?*

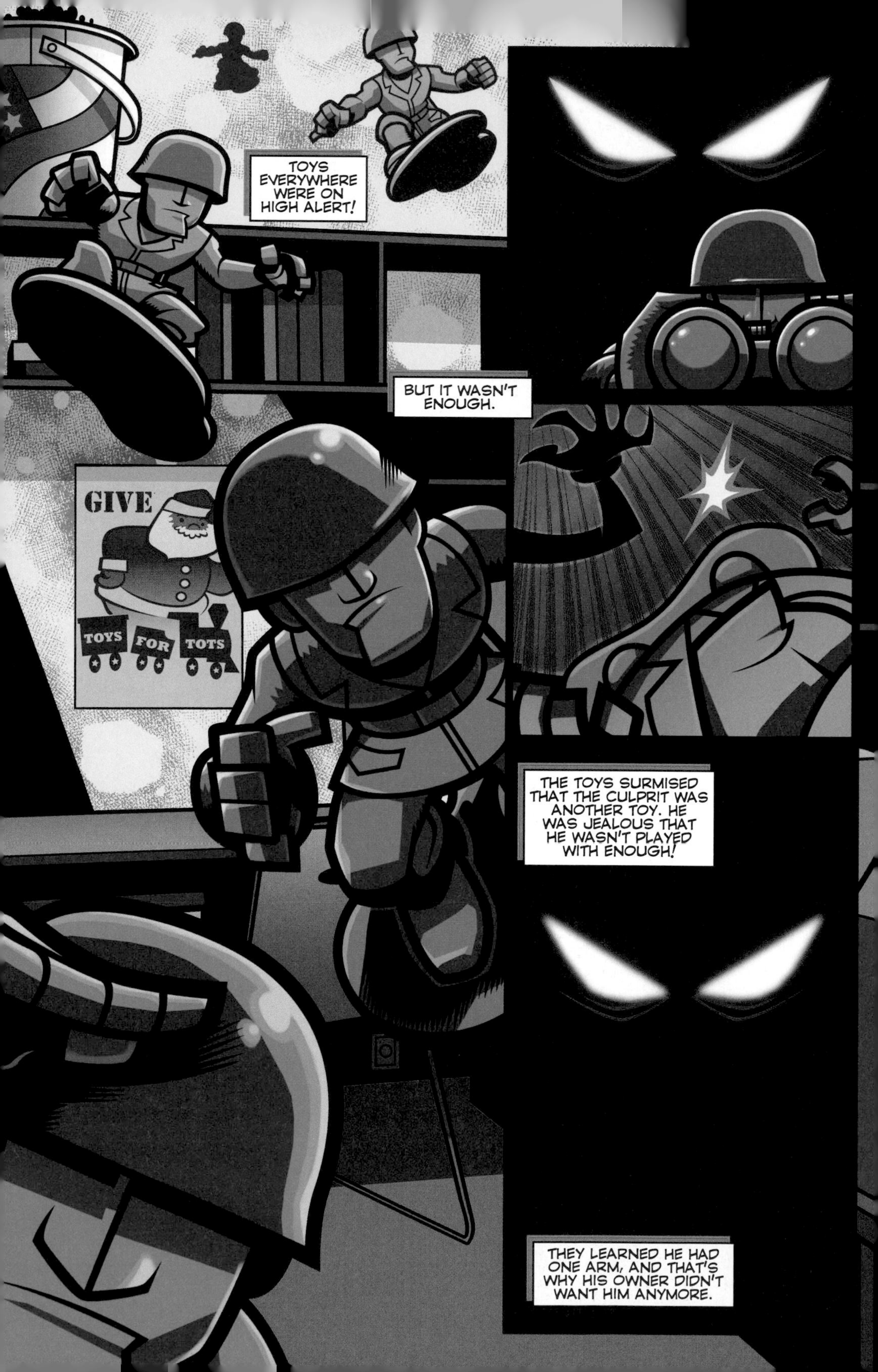
TOYS EVERYWHERE WERE ON HIGH ALERT!
BUT IT WASN'T ENOUGH.
GIVE
TOYS FOR TOTS
THE TOYS SURMISED THAT THE CULPRIT WAS ANOTHER TOY. HE WAS JEALOUS THAT HE WASN'T PLAYED WITH ENOUGH!
THEY LEARNED HE HAD ONE ARM, AND THAT'S WHY HIS OWNER DIDN'T WANT HIM ANYMORE.

ONE DAY THE ONE-ARMED TOY TAKER JUST DISAPPEARED. THE TOYS WERE SAFE AGAIN.
福
BUT HE'S STILL OUT THERE. WAITING. WATCHING. PICKING HIS MOMENT TO STRIKE...
AND I KNOW THIS BECAUSE...
福
I AM THE ONE-ARMED MONSTER!
HAHAHAHAHA!

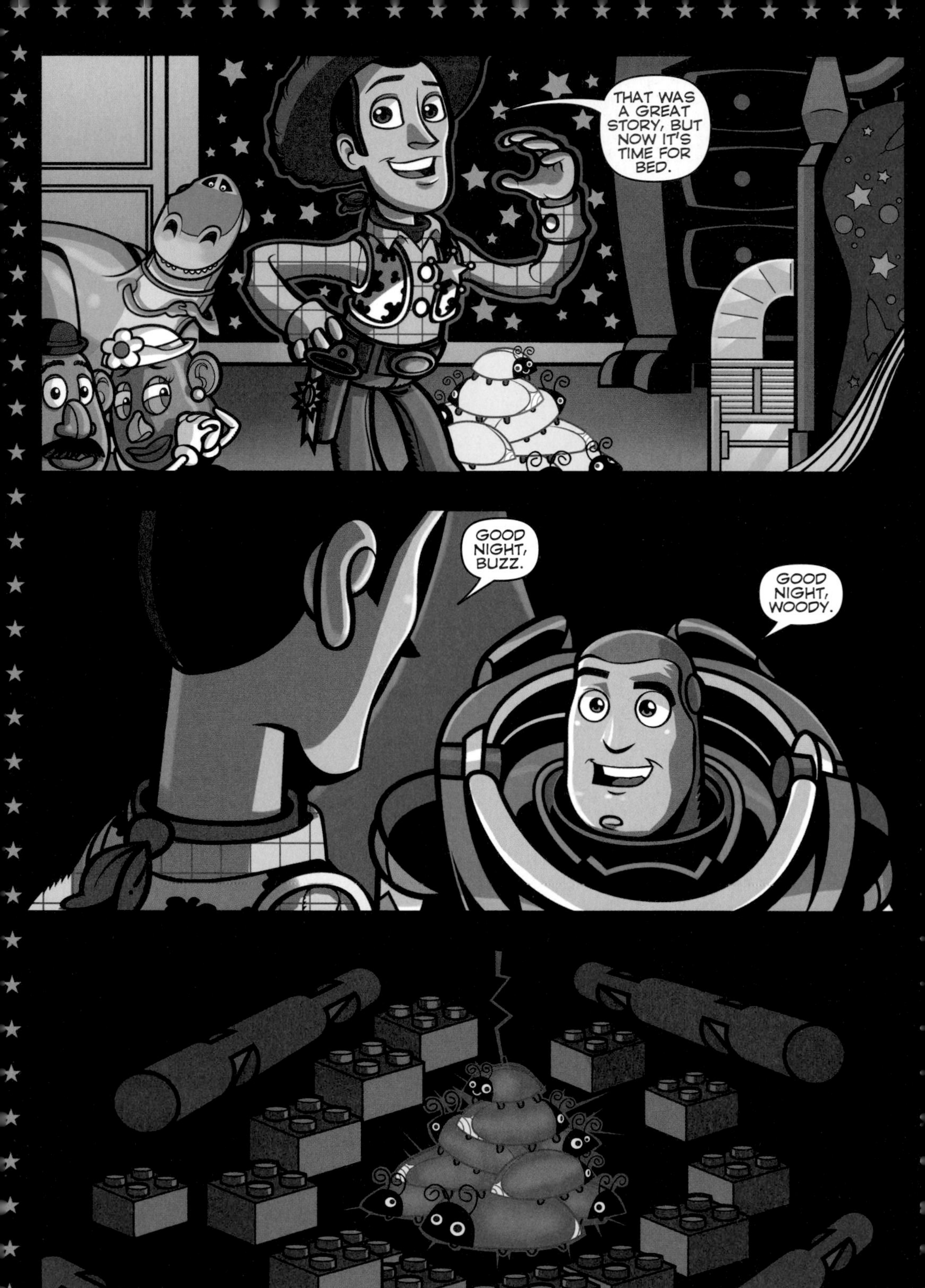
THAT WAS A GREAT STORY, BUT NOW IT'S TIME FOR BED.
GOOD NIGHT, BUZZ.
GOOD NIGHT, WOODY.

GRRRRRRRRRRRRRRRRR
HEY, BUZZ, YOU HEAR THAT?
YEAH. IT SOUNDED LIKE IT WAS COMING FROM UNDER ANDY'S BED.
IT'S PROBABLY REX OR POTATO HEAD JUST TRYING TO SCARE US.
IT'S NOT US!

LET'S GET TO THE BOTTOM OF THIS.

SNARRL
GROWWL GRR

WHOA!
HOLD ON, WOODY!
GRRRRRRR
WWROROROLLLLL
WHATEVER'S UNDER THERE ISN'T IN A GOOD MOOD.
HMMM. IT APPEARS THAT SOME KIND OF CANINE CHEWED UP THIS STICK.
THAT CAN ONLY MEAN--
BUSTER!
EH, I DON'T THINK SO. BUSTER'S OUTSIDE.

VRRRRRRREEEEMM
VROOM
GOOD IDEA, RC. A FLASHLIGHT!
GRRRROWWWWLLLL
GRRRRRRR
SHOW YOURSELF, MONSTER!
WOOF
WOOF
WOOF

AHHHHHHHHHH!
HAHAHA! BOY HOWDY, I GOT YOU ALL GOOD!
YOU SURE DID, SLINK!
WELL DONE.
I THINK THAT'S ENOUGH SCARING FOR ONE NIGHT.
ME TOO! I DON'T THINK I COULD TAKE ANYMORE. I'M GOING TO BED!
THE END

CHECK OUT THESE EXCLUSIVE PREVIEWS OF OTHER GREAT TITLES NOW AVAILABLE FROM

BOOM KIDS!

It's a battle of the Buzzes when Andy gets an unexpected present... another Buzz Lightyear?

TOY STORY: THE RETURN OF BUZZ LIGHTYEAR
DIAMOND CODE: JAN100839
SC $9.99 ISBN 9781608865574
HC $24.99 ISBN 9781608865581

ANDY, HOW MANY TIMES HAVE I TOLD YOU NOT TO RUN DOWN THE STAIRS?!
SORRY, MOM.

WHAT'S A "GIFT RECEIPT"? AND WHAT DOES SHE MEAN "RETURN IT AND GET SOMETHING NEW?" YOU CAN DO THAT?!
YEAH, BUZZ...YOU CAN.
THAT JUST SEEMS... WRONG.
IT'S LIKE THE POOR TOY NEVER EVEN HAD A CHANCE...

TRUST ME BUZZ...IT'S FOR THE BEST.
"FOR THE BEST?" I THOUGHT YOU'D BE ON MY SIDE.
I AM ON YOUR SIDE.
OBVIOUSLY NOT, WOODY.

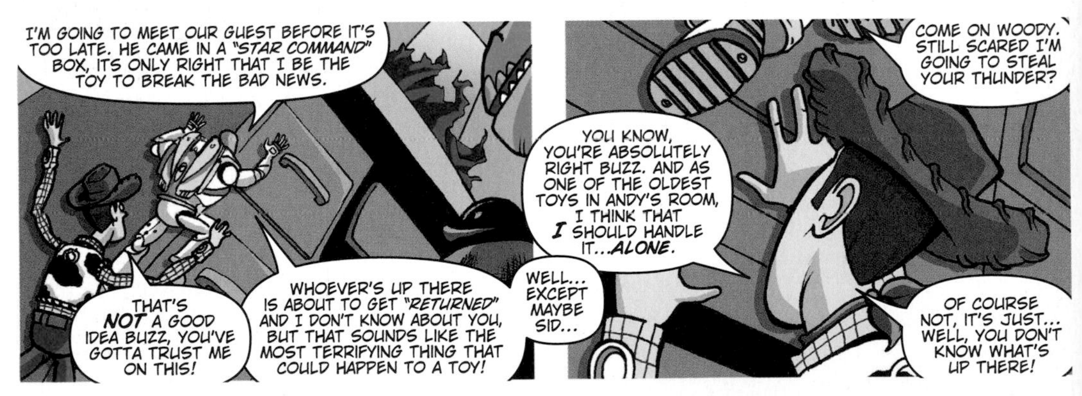
I'M GOING TO MEET OUR GUEST BEFORE IT'S TOO LATE. HE CAME IN A "STAR COMMAND" BOX, ITS ONLY RIGHT THAT I BE THE TOY TO BREAK THE BAD NEWS.
THAT'S NOT A GOOD IDEA BUZZ, YOU'VE GOTTA TRUST ME ON THIS!
WHOEVER'S UP THERE IS ABOUT TO GET "RETURNED" AND I DON'T KNOW ABOUT YOU, BUT THAT SOUNDS LIKE THE MOST TERRIFYING THING THAT COULD HAPPEN TO A TOY!
WELL... EXCEPT MAYBE SID...
COME ON WOODY. STILL SCARED I'M GOING TO STEAL YOUR THUNDER?
OF COURSE NOT, IT'S JUST... WELL, YOU DON'T KNOW WHAT'S UP THERE!
YOU KNOW, YOU'RE ABSOLUTELY RIGHT BUZZ. AND AS ONE OF THE OLDEST TOYS IN ANDY'S ROOM, I THINK THAT I SHOULD HANDLE IT...ALONE.

YOU'RE RIGHT. THAT'S WHY I'M GOING UP THERE TO FIND OUT!
OH...

BUZZ LIGHTYEAR
SPACE RANGER
I CAN REALLY BE DENSE, CAN'T I?
ON THAT WE CAN AGREE.
STILL WANT TO MEET HIM?
I FEEL LIKE I ALREADY KNOW HIM.
LET ME TALK TO HIM WOODY... SPACE RANGER TO SPACE RANGER.

TERRAIN LOOKS STABLE. CAN'T DETERMINE YET WHETHER THE ATMOSPHERE IS BREATHABLE. AND THERE SEEMS TO BE NO SIGN OF INTELLIGENT LIFE ANYWHERE.

HALT!
IDENTIFY YOURSELF!
HELLO!
BZZ-ZZZ-ZZZZZ
HEY! WHOA THERE SOLDIER!
SORRY! I DIDN'T MEAN TO STARTLE YOU.
MY NAME...IS BUZZ AND THIS IS...ANDY'S ROOM.
I COME IN PEACE.

... WERE YOU SAYING SOMETHING? I COULDN'T HEAR YOU OVER THE LASER...
I SAID... I COME IN PEACE!

AS DO I! SORRY ABOUT THE LASER, FRIEND!
THE NAME'S BUZZ LIGHTYEAR: SPACE RANGER, U.P.U.
THAT'S THE UNIVERSE PROTECTION UNIT.
YEAH... I KNOW. LOOK, YOU REALLY AREN'T SUPPOSED TO BE OUT OF YOUR PACKAGE.
IT'S CALLED A "STARSHIP." WHAT'S YOUR DESIGNATION, RANGER?
BUZZ... BUZZ LIGHTYEAR.
WELL, THAT'S JUST GOING TO BE CONFUSING. WHY DON'T WE JUST CALL YOU "SALLY?"
YOU'VE GOT TO BE KIDDING.

Disney · PIXAR
THE INCREDIBLES
SECRETS & LIES
BOOM KIDS!

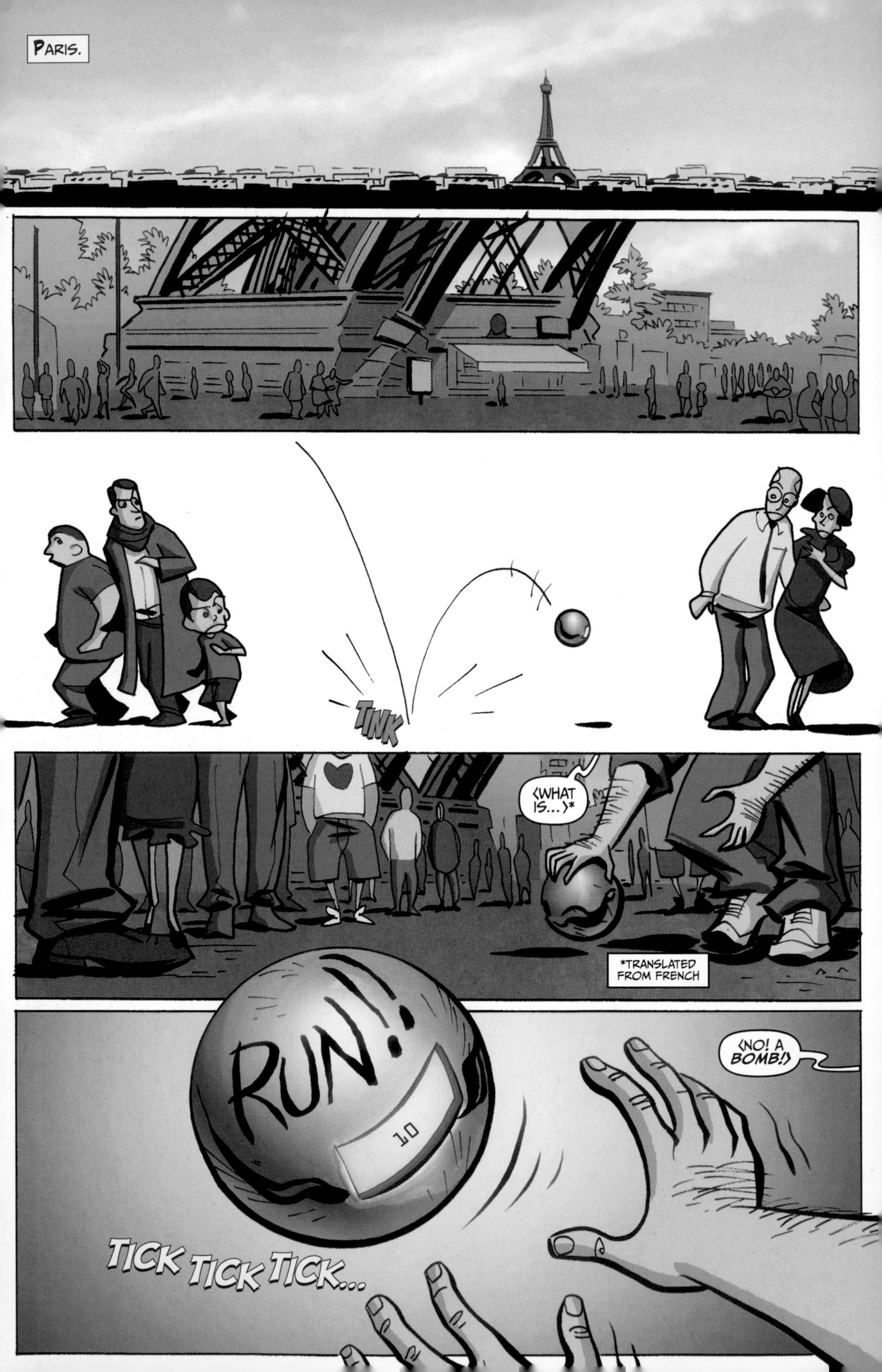
PARIS.
TINK
⟨WHAT IS...⟩*
*TRANSLATED FROM FRENCH
RUN!!
10
⟨NO! A BOMB!⟩
TICK TICK TICK...

THE MUNICIBERG HERALD
EIFFEL TOWER ATTACKED!
Lorem ipsum dolor sit amet, consectetur adipisicing elit, sed do eiusmod tempor incididunt ut labore et dolore magna aliqua. Ut enim ad minim veniam, quis nostrud exercitation ullamco laboris nisi ut aliquip ex ea commodo consequat. Duis aute irure dolor in reprehenderit in voluptate velit esse cillum dolore eu fugiat nulla pariatur. Excepteur sint occaecat cupidatat non proident, sunt in culpa qui officia deserunt mollit anim id est laborum.
PRIME MINISTER CONSIDERS SURRENDER
POLICE SEEK "BOMB VOYAGE" AS PRIMARY SUSPECT
BOMB VOYAGE? TALK ABOUT A BLAST FROM THE PAST. I HAVEN'T THOUGHT OF HIM IN *YEARS...*

HE WAS NEVER *CAUGHT.* DISAPPEARED WHEN ALL THE HEROES WENT UNDERGROUND. NOW THAT *YOU'RE ALL* BACK...

THIS IS A MESS. THE EIFFEL TOWER...IT'S JUST...*GONE.* ATOMIZED IN THE *BLINK OF AN EYE.*
RICK...I THINK WE SHOULD CALL BOB. HE FOUGHT BOMB VOYAGE MORE TIMES THAN I CAN REMEMBER. HE *KNOWS* HIM.

NO... AND *BEFORE* YOU ARGUE, I'VE GOT TWO REASONS. *NEITHER* OF WHICH YOU'RE GOING TO *LIKE.*

ALL RIGHT.

BELINDA? SEND IN MY 2 O'CLOCK.
BZZZ!

THIS SITUATION IS MORE COMPLICATED THAN YOU CAN POSSIBLY IMAGINE. SO I NEED YOU TO TRUST ME.
WELL, THAT'S A LITTLE CRYPTIC. C'MON, RICK, WE'VE KNOWN EACH OTHER FOR--

FSSH
AGENT DICKER. MRS. PARR.

AH. I SEE.

HELEN... LISTEN. THIS *IS* A VOLATILE SITUATION...
YOU HAVE NO IDEA HOW AWARE I AM OF THAT, RICK.

THE ***GOVERNMENT*** IN FRANCE HAS FORMALLY ASKED FOR OUR ***INTERVENTION...***
THAT'S GOOD. I'M GLAD.

AND MIRAGE *IS* A KEY AGENT IN THE INVESTIGATION. WE ***NEED*** HER...
FINE. THAT'S FINE.

SO MAYBE YOU SHOULD ***STOP*** STRANGLING HER NOW.

OF COURSE.

-KAFF!- -GASP!-
ARE YOU SERIOUS, RICK? YOU EXPECT ME TO WORK WITH HER? AFTER WHAT SHE ALMOST DID TO MY FAMILY?
YES I DO, HELEN. AND HERE'S THE REASON...

WHAT IS IT, RICK?
-KAFF KAFF-

XEREK. XEREK IS BACK.

The MUPPET SHOW©
Comic Book
BANG

The MUPPET SHO

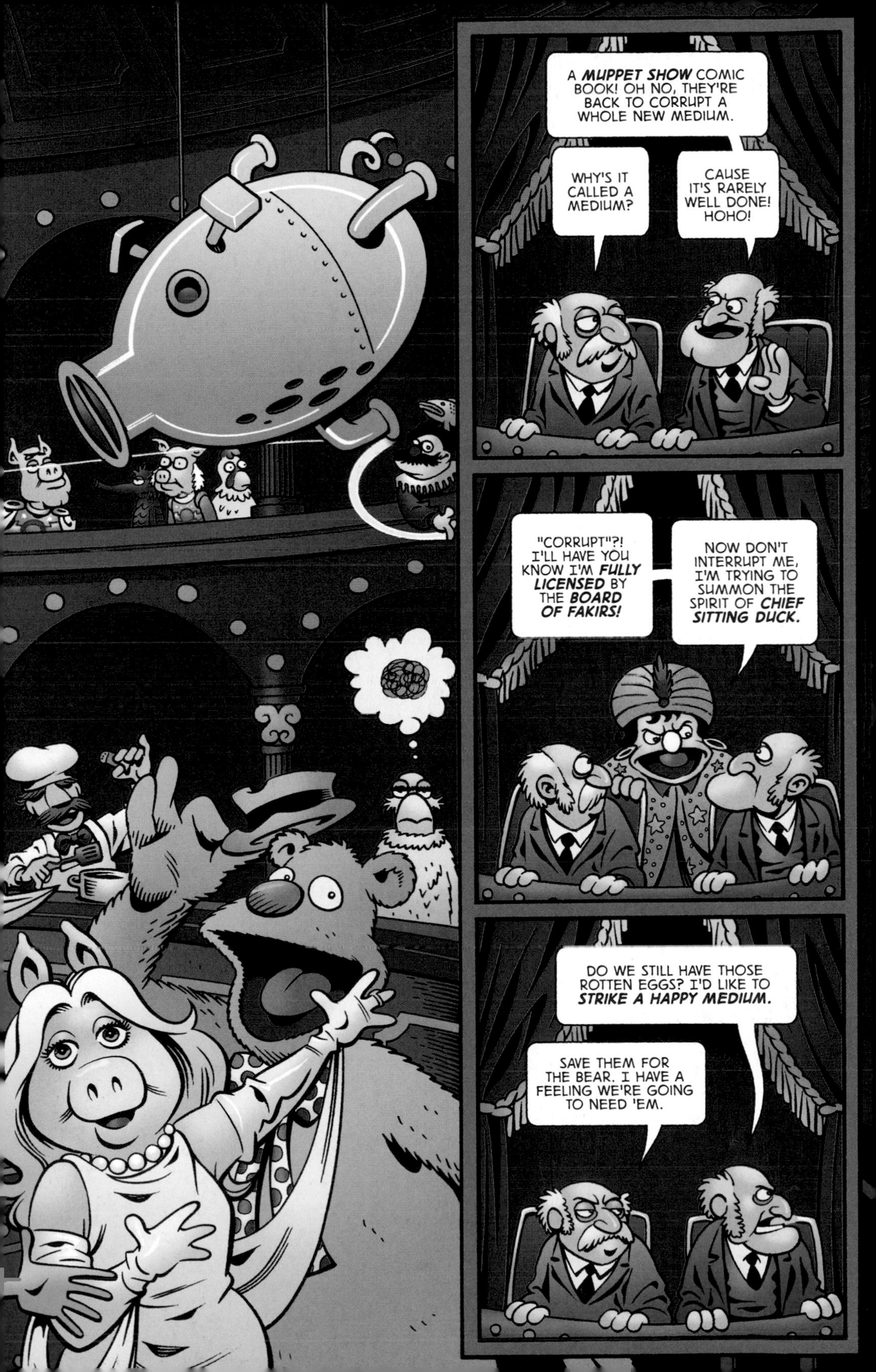

A MUPPET SHOW COMIC BOOK! OH NO, THEY'RE BACK TO CORRUPT A WHOLE NEW MEDIUM.
WHY'S IT CALLED A MEDIUM?
CAUSE IT'S RARELY WELL DONE! HOHO!
"CORRUPT"?! I'LL HAVE YOU KNOW I'M FULLY LICENSED BY THE BOARD OF FAKIRS!
NOW DON'T INTERRUPT ME, I'M TRYING TO SUMMON THE SPIRIT OF CHIEF SITTING DUCK.
DO WE STILL HAVE THOSE ROTTEN EGGS? I'D LIKE TO STRIKE A HAPPY MEDIUM.
SAVE THEM FOR THE BEAR. I HAVE A FEELING WE'RE GOING TO NEED 'EM.

AND NOW IT'S TIME FOR...
VETERINARIAN'S HOSPITAL
THE CONTINUING STORY OF A QUACK WHO'S GONE TO THE DOGS!
ALL RIGHT, NURSE JANICE...WHAT'S THE DIAGNOSIS?
IT'S, LIKE, THAT THING YOU DO WHEN YOU TRY TO WORK OUT WHAT'S WRONG WITH THE PATIENT?
BOY, ARE YOU IN THE WRONG PROFESSION!

HMM...WELL, YOU SEEM TO BE ALL RIGHT APART FROM A FEW MINOR BURNS, A BROKEN NECK, A CONCUSSION AND WATER ON THE BRAIN.
OH, AND BY THE WAY-- IT'S TWINS!
YAWHODATHEWHA?

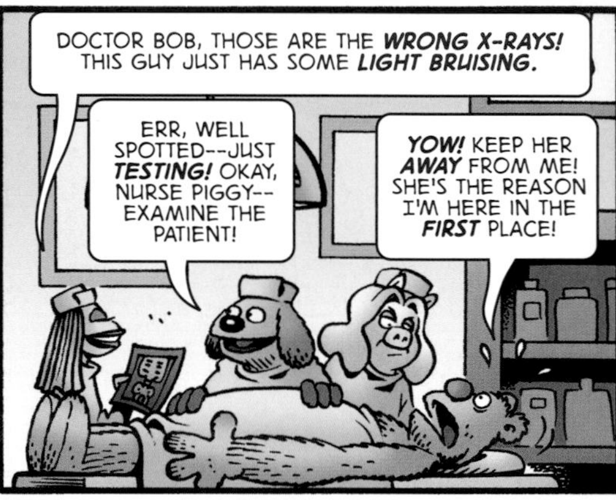
DOCTOR BOB, THOSE ARE THE WRONG X-RAYS! THIS GUY JUST HAS SOME LIGHT BRUISING.
ERR, WELL SPOTTED--JUST TESTING! OKAY, NURSE PIGGY-- EXAMINE THE PATIENT!
YOW! KEEP HER AWAY FROM ME! SHE'S THE REASON I'M HERE IN THE FIRST PLACE!

NURSE PIGGY! IS THIS TRUE?
MY HANDS SLIPPED.
THIRTY-SEVEN TIMES?!
I'M VERY CLUMSY.
GREAT! WELL, NO EVIDENCE OF MALPRACTICE HERE! WE'LL HAVE YOU BACK PLAYING THAT VIOLIN IN NO TIME!

BUT...BUT I DON'T PLAY THE VIOLIN.
OH. IN THAT CASE, YOU'VE ONLY GOT THREE DAYS TO LIVE!

HA HAHA HAHA HA
I'M JUST KIDDING! I GIVE YOU AT LEAST A MONTH!

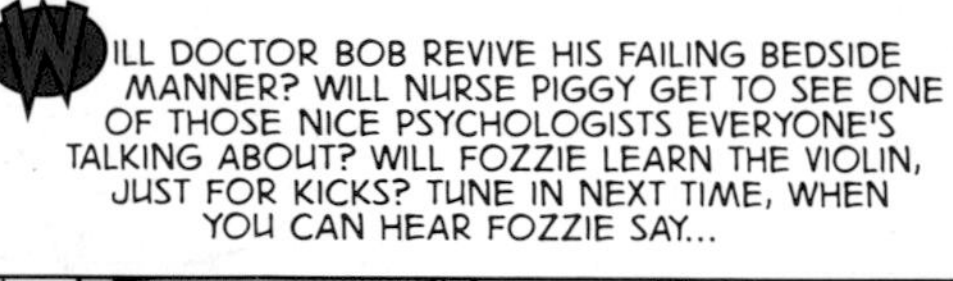
WILL DOCTOR BOB REVIVE HIS FAILING BEDSIDE MANNER? WILL NURSE PIGGY GET TO SEE ONE OF THOSE NICE PSYCHOLOGISTS EVERYONE'S TALKING ABOUT? WILL FOZZIE LEARN THE VIOLIN, JUST FOR KICKS? TUNE IN NEXT TIME, WHEN YOU CAN HEAR FOZZIE SAY...

SO TELL ME STRAIGHT, DOC... WILL I BE OKAY?
YOU'LL BE FINE...BUT THOSE TWINS ARE GOING TO KEEP YOU UP ALL NIGHT!

HMM...MOTHER OF PEARL EFFECT ON PLUMAGE...NOPE. LAYS EGGS IN SWAMP WATER... NOPE. HE **CAN'T** BE A SPARROW...
SCOOTER! WHAT'S UP?
ORNITHOLOGY FOR THE EXCEEDINGLY DIM

RIZZO! TELL ME...DO YOU KNOW GONZO'S **SPECIES?** IT'S REALLY, REALLY IMPORTANT!
CAN'T SAY AS I DO, SPORT. I **CAN** TELL YOU HE'S DEFINITELY NOT A **COW.**

NOT A C-O... **AARGH!** WHAT AM I **DOING?!**
MAYBE YOU SHOULD JUST, LIKE, **OBSERVE FROM A DISTANCE.** HE'S BOUND TO DO SOMETHING **SPECIES-SPECIFIC** SOONER OR LATER...

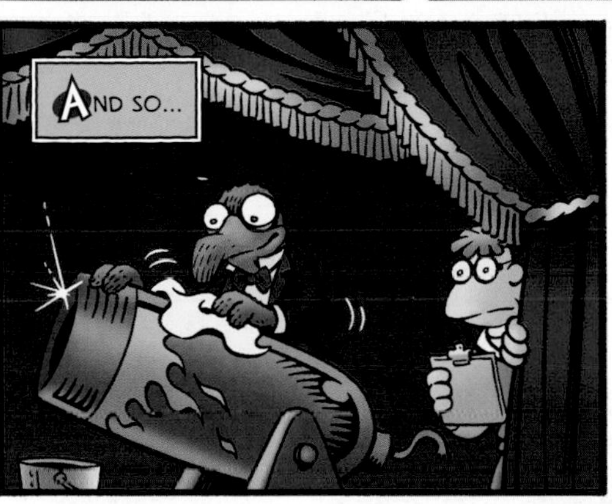
AND SO...

WHAT DO *YOU* THINK GONZO IS?

HOËR BÜRK DER ÜMLÅÜT ÜRN DER BØËKY-BØËK?

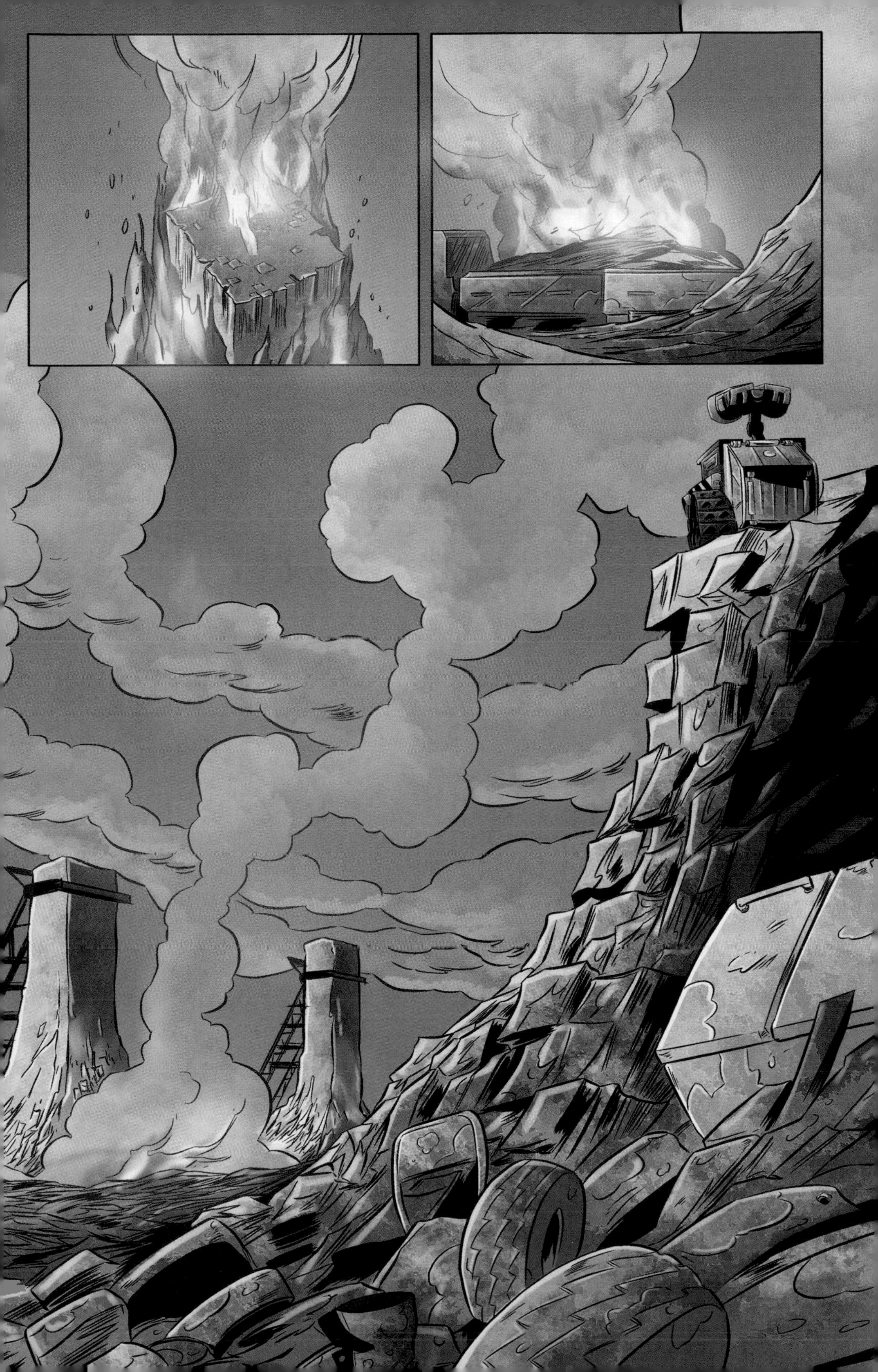

KLIK
BWOOOMM

KLIK
BWOOOMM

KLIK
BWOOOMM

HMMM?

SLAM

D-DUH
D-DUH
D-DUH

...

!

...whoa...

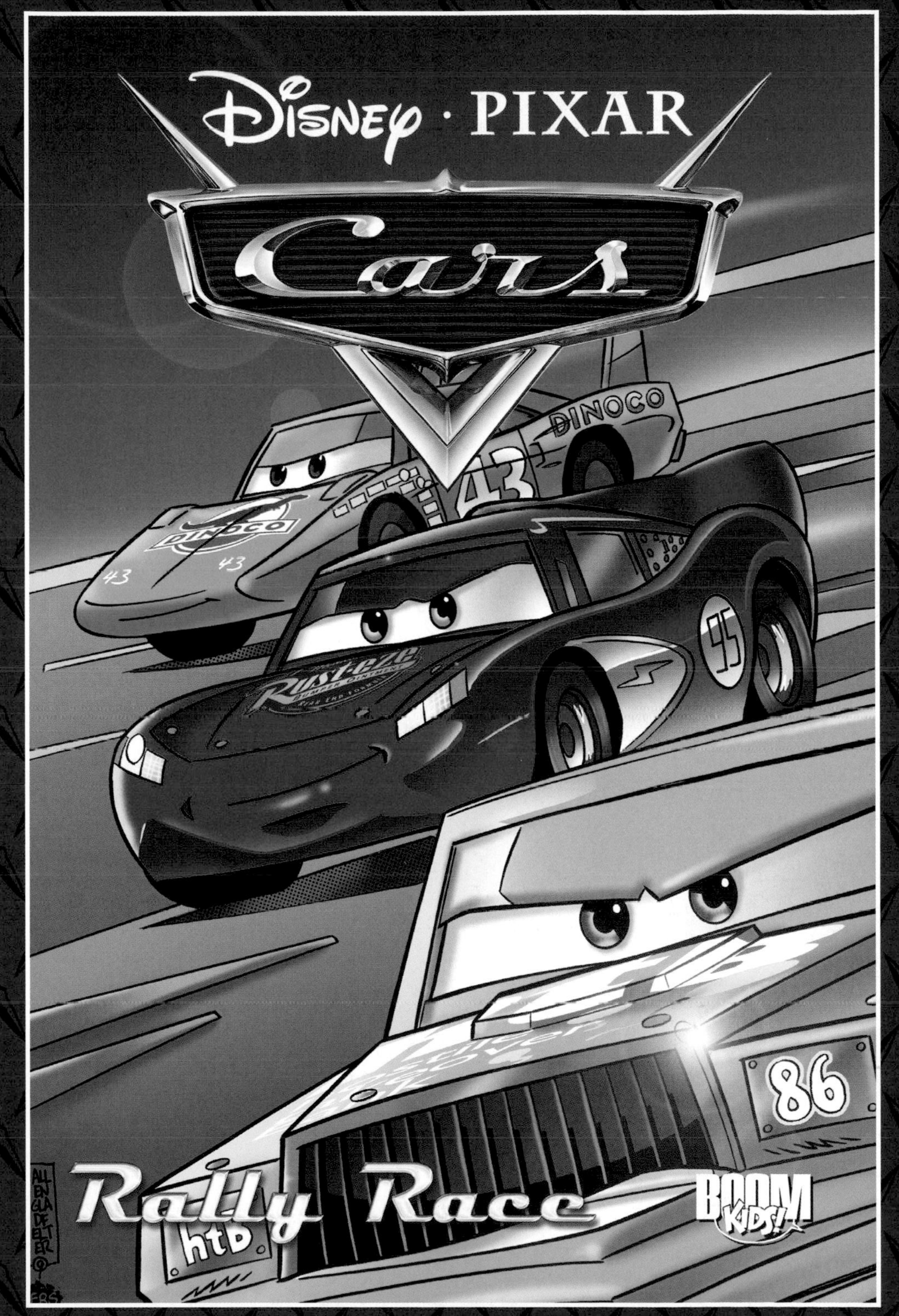
Disney · PIXAR
Cars
DINOCO
43
Rust-eze
95
86
Rally Race
htb
BOOM KIDS!

FOGGY WINDSHIELD
LUBEORAMA
THE OIL PAN CAFE
POP N PATCH TIRE REPAIR
OH YEAH, *BRING IT ON,* BOYS!
KAFF! KAFF!
THAT'S A BAD HABIT YOU HAVE THERE, MULVILL.

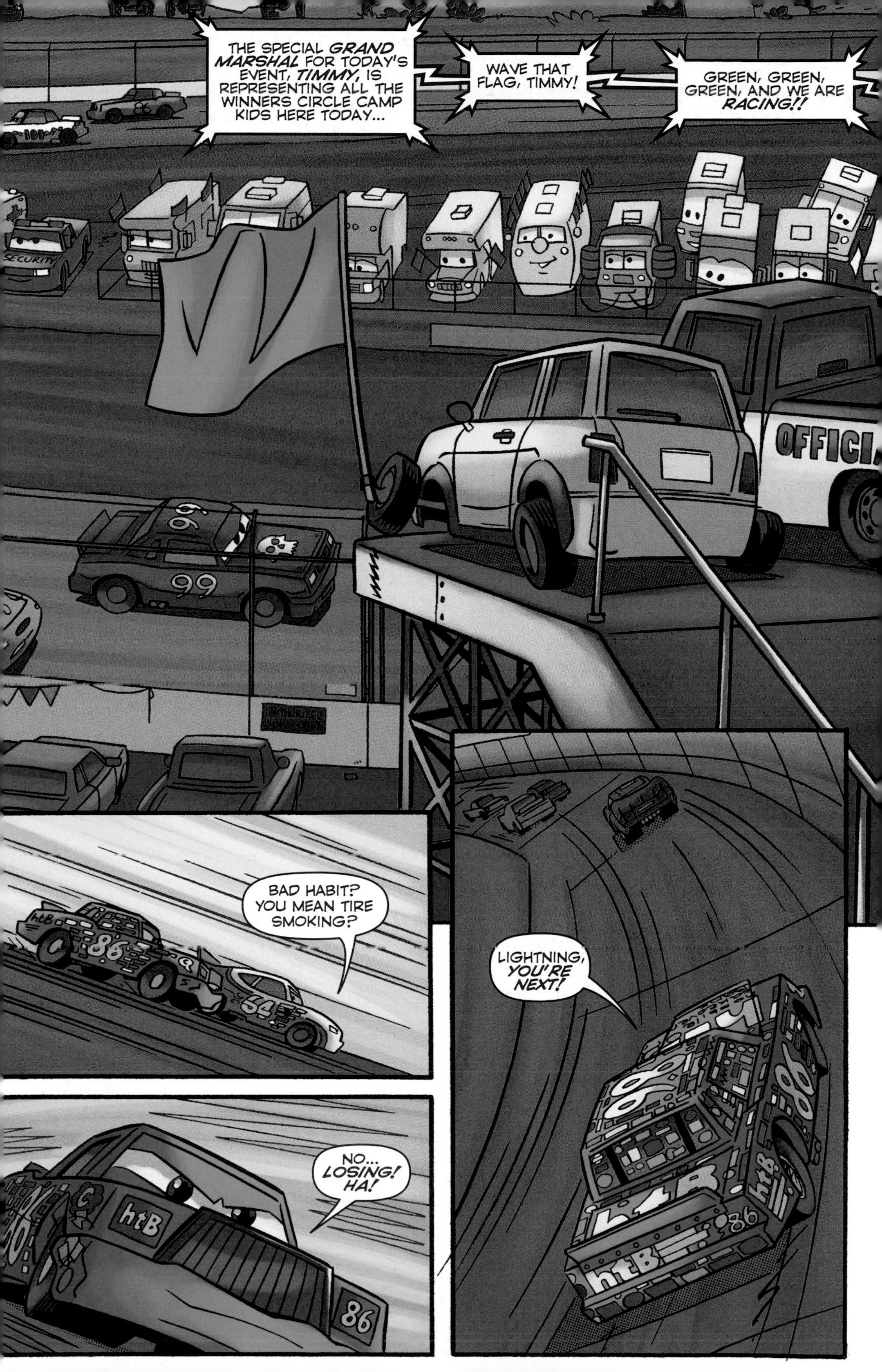
THE SPECIAL GRAND MARSHAL FOR TODAY'S EVENT, TIMMY, IS REPRESENTING ALL THE WINNERS CIRCLE CAMP KIDS HERE TODAY...
WAVE THAT FLAG, TIMMY!
GREEN, GREEN, GREEN, AND WE ARE RACING!!
SECURITY
OFFICI
99
BAD HABIT? YOU MEAN TIRE SMOKING?
NO... LOSING! HA!
LIGHTNING, YOU'RE NEXT!

NICE MOVE, LIGHTNING, BUT IT WON'T MATTER... CHICK'S COMIN' FOR YA!

SEE YA LATER, CANDYMAN.

YOU CAN RUN, LIGHTNING...

...BUT YOU CAN'T HIDE!

WHAT'S THE MATTER, MR. BIGTIME TV ANNOUNCER? NOTHING TO SAY?
MAYBE YOU'RE GETTING A LITTLE TOO OLD TO RUN WITH THE BIG BOYS, EH, CARTRIP?

YOUR TIME WILL COME, HICKS, YOUR TIME WILL COME!
NO, MY TIME IS NOW! KA-CHIGGA!

YOU LEFT ME AN OPENING, BOYS...
...YOU BETTER BELIEVE I'M GONNA GO FOR IT!
BANG!
WHOA!

WAH!! YOU CLUMSY OAF, HICKS!
SCREECH!!

LIGHTNING MCQUEEN CLOSES THE GAP WITH ANDRETTI, WITH CHICK HICKS HOT ON HIS TAIL...
SORRY, MARIO.
IT'S ALL GOOD, LIGHTNING! SEE YOU AT THE FINISH LINE.
LEGEND OR NOT, IT'S TIME FOR YOU TO *MOVE OVER,* OLD MAN.
YOU'VE GOT NO CLASS, YOU KNOW THAT, HICKS?
NO CLASS? WELL, I JUST *SCHOOLED* YOU! *HA!*

I'M RIGHT BEHIND YOU, LIGHTNING!
htB hostile takeover Bank
86

OKAY, CHICK, TIME TO GET NEW TIRES. *PIT NOW.*

YOU'VE HAD A STAY OF EXECUTION, LIGHTNING!

The Muppet Show Comic Book
BANG
THE MUPPET SHOW COMIC BOOK: MEET THE MUPPETS
Collecting the first four issues of the Eisner Award-nominated THE MUPPET SHOW COMIC BOOK, written and drawn by the incomparable Roger Langridge! Packed full of madcap skits and gags, this trade is certain to please old and new fans alike!
SC $9.99 ISBN 9781934506851
HC $24.99 ISBN 9781608865277
THE MUPPET SHOW COMIC BOOK: THE TREASURE OF PEG-LEG WILSON
Scooter discovers old documents which reveal that a cache of treasure is hidden somewhere within the Muppet Theater...and when Rizzo the Rat overhears this, the news spreads like wildfire! Can Kermit keep everyone from tearing the theater apart?
SC $9.99 ISBN 9781608865048
HC $24.99 ISBN 9781608865307
THE MUPPET SHOW COMIC BOOK: ON THE ROAD
With the Muppet Theater destroyed, the Muppets take their act on the road...but with two very familiar hecklers in every town, will the show be a hit, or will our Muppet minstrels be run out of town in tar and feathers? Also: PIGS IN SPACE!
SC $9.99 ISBN 9781608865161
The Muppet Show Comic Book
ON THE ROAD
The Muppet Show Comic Book
BOOM! KIDS!
THE TREASURE OF PEG-LEG WILSON
Disney • PIXAR
THE WORLD OF
Cars
The Rooki
Rust-eze
95
CARS: THE ROOKIE
See how Lightning McQueen became a Piston Cup sensation! CARS: THE ROOKIE reveals Lightning McQueen's scrappy origins as a local short track racer who dreams of the big time... and recklessly plows his way through the competition to get there!
SC $9.99 ISBN 9781934506844
HC $24.99 ISBN 9781608865222
CARS: RADIATOR SPRINGS
Lightning McQueen is hanging out with his friends at Flo's V8 Café when he realizes that everyone knows his story...but he doesn't know anyone else's! Lightning wants to know how his friends ended up in Radiator Springs...and more importantly, why they decided to stay!
SC $9.99 ISBN 9781608865024
HC $24.99 ISBN 9781608865284
Disney • PIXAR
THE WORLD OF
Cars

WALL•E: RECHARGE

Before WALL•E becomes the hardworking robot we know and love, he lets the few remaining robots take care of the trash compacting while he collects interesting junk. But when these robots start breaking down, WALL•E must adjust his priorities...or else Earth is doomed!

SC $9.99 ISBN 9781608865123
HC $24.99 ISBN 9781608865543

MUPPET ROBIN HOOD

The Muppets tell the Robin Hood legend for laughs, and it's the reader who will be merry! Robin Hood (Kermit the Frog) joins with the Merry Men, Sherwood Forest's infamous gang of misfit outlaws, to take on the Sheriff of Nottingham (Sam the Eagle)!

SC $9.99 ISBN 9781934506790
HC $24.99 ISBN 9781608865260

MUPPET PETER PAN

When Peter Pan (Kermit) whisks Wendy (Janice) and her brothers to Neverswamp, the adventure begins! With Captain Hook (Gonzo) out for revenge for the loss of his hand, can even the magic of Piggytink (Miss Piggy) save Wendy and her brothers?

SC $9.99 ISBN 9781608865079
HC $24.99 ISBN 9781608865314

FINDING NEMO: REEF RESCUE

Nemo, Dory and Marlin have become local heroes, and are recruited to embark on an all-new adventure in this exciting collection! The reef is mysteriously dying and no one knows why. So Nemo and his friends must travel the great blue sea to save their home!

SC $9.99 ISBN 9781934506882
HC $24.99 ISBN 9781608865246

MONSTERS, INC.: LAUGH FACTORY

Someone is stealing comedy props from the other employees, making it difficult for them to harvest the laughter they need to power Monstropolis...and all evidence points to Sulley's best friend Mike Wazowski!

SC $9.99 ISBN 9781608865086
HC $24.99 ISBN 9781608865338

DISNEY'S HERO SQUAD: ULTRAHEROES VOL. 1: SAVE THE WORLD

It's an all-star cast of your favorite Disney characters, as you have never seen them before. Join Donald Duck, Goofy, Daisy, and even Mickey himself as they defend the fate of the planet as the one and only Ultraheroes!

SC $9.99 ISBN 9781608865437
HC $24.99 ISBN 9781608865529

UNCLE SCROOGE: THE HUNT FOR THE OLD NUMBER ONE

Join Donald Duck's favorite penny-pinching Uncle Scrooge as he, Donald himself and Huey, Dewey, and Louie embark on a globe-spanning trek to recover treasure and save Scrooge's "number one dime" from the treacherous Magica De Spell.

SC $9.99 ISBN 9781608865475
HC $24.99 ISBN 9781608865536

WIZARDS OF MICKEY VOL. 1: MOUSE MAGIC

Your favorite Disney characters star in this magical fantasy epic! Student of the great wizard Nereus, Mickey allies himself with Donald and team mate Goofy, in a quest to find a magical crown that will give him mastery over all spells!

SC $9.99 ISBN 9781608865413
HC $24.99 ISBN 9781608865505

DONALD DUCK AND FRIENDS: DOUBLE DUCK VOL. 1

Donald Duck as a secret agent? Villainous fiends beware as the world of super sleuthing and espionage will never be the same! This is Donald Duck like you've never seen him!

SC $9.99 ISBN 9781608865451
HC $24.99 ISBN 9781608865512

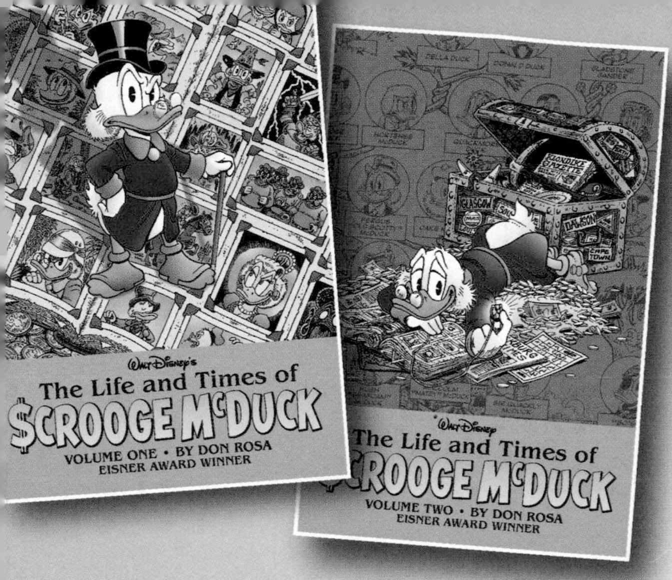

THE LIFE AND TIMES OF SCROOGE McDUCK VOL. 1

BOOM Kids! proudly collects the first half of THE LIFE AND TIMES OF SCROOGE MCDUCK in a gorgeous hardcover collection – featuring smyth sewn binding, a gold-on-gold foil-stamped case wrap, and a bookmark ribbon! These stories, written and drawn by legendary cartoonist Don Rosa, chronicle Scrooge McDuck's fascinating life.

HC $24.99 ISBN 9781608865383

THE LIFE AND TIMES OF SCROOGE McDUCK VOL. 2

BOOM Kids! proudly presents volume two of THE LIFE AND TIMES OF SCROOGE MCDUCK in a gorgeous hardcover collection in a beautiful, deluxe package featuring smyth sewn binding and a foil-stamped case wrap! These stories, written and drawn by legendary cartoonist Don Rosa, chronicle Scrooge McDuck's fascinating life.

HC $24.99 ISBN 9781608865420

MICKEY MOUSE CLASSICS: MOUSE TAILS

See Mickey Mouse as he was meant to be seen! Solving mysteries, fighting off pirates, and generally saving the day! These classic stories comprise a "Greatest Hits" series for the mouse, including a story produced by seminal Disney creator Carl Barks!

HC $24.99 ISBN 9781608865390

DONALD DUCK CLASSICS: QUACK UP

Whether it's finding gold, journeying to the Klondike, or fighting ghosts, Donald will always have the help of his much more prepared nephews – Huey, Dewey, and Louie – by his side. Featuring some of the best Donald Duck stories Carl Barks ever produced!

HC $24.99 ISBN 9781608865406

Walt Disney's Valentine's Classics

Walt Disney's CHRISTMAS CLASSICS

WALT DISNEY'S VALENTINE'S CLASSICS

Love is in the air for Mickey Mouse, Donald Duck and the rest of the gang. But will Cupid's arrows cause happiness or heartache? Find out in this collection of classic stories featuring work by Carl Barks, Floyd Gottfredson, Daan Jippes, Romano Scarpa and Al Taliaferro.

HC $24.99 ISBN 9781608865499

WALT DISNEY'S CHRISTMAS CLASSICS

BOOM Kids! has raided the Disney publishing archives and searched every nook and cranny to find the best and the greatest Christmas stories from Disney's vast comic book publishing history for this "best of" compilation.

HC $24.99 ISBN 9781608865482